COWBOYS & MISTLETOE

A STARLIGHT SWEET ROMANCE

JACQUELINE WINTERS

Cowboys & Mistletoe is a work of fiction. Names, characters, businesses, places, events, and incidents are either the products of the author's imagination or used in a fictitious manner. Any resemblance to actual persons, living or dead, or actual events is purely coincidental.

Editor: Bridge to Story

Copy Editor: Write Girl Editing Services

Cover Design: Brennylou Designs

Proofreading: FictionEdit.com

Created with Vellum

CHAPTER 1

Holly

Holly Maxwell leaned against a rickety table in the old barn, praying it wouldn't fall apart with her weight. She'd spent the last hour inside the cold structure, searching for inspiration, hopeful some idea would pop out at her. The key to reversing the ranch's financial position had to lie in this big old barn. Her gut told her it did anyway.

"I don't know, guys," she said to her dog, Blitzen, and his unlikely best friend, Norbert. They stood side by side, blinking back at her, the white golden retriever and the black Angus calf. "Am I wasting my time out here?"

The brainstorming list she began an hour ago

had transformed into a cleaning list when practical ideas failed to fill the page. At least cleaning would give her some sense of accomplishment. Some sense of *doing* something, even if it ultimately wouldn't add to the bottom line.

Move garden tools to the new shed.

Move hay bales to the loft of the main barn.

Sweep floors.

Sweep them again.

Relocate tractor.

Since she had been a little girl growing up on the Maxwell Ranch, she'd always fantasized that this big red barn could be transformed into so many things. But the whimsical ideas of a child hardly aligned with the realities of an adult, years later now that she was the appointed ranch manager. "Can't exactly turn it into a castle, now, can I?"

Blitzen and Norbert tilted their heads in unison. The pair had been inseparable since Holly was forced to bottle-feed the calf when his mother wouldn't claim him earlier that spring.

Clean windows.

For the last year, her grandparents had left her to manage the family ranch, the largest and most successful one in the county. Grandma Charlotte had insisted she and Grandpa travel the year together in an RV. Before they departed, they gave Holly a chance to test the knowledge Grandpa'd instilled in her over the years. Too bad it'd been their worst financial year in two decades.

"Might as well take the F now," she muttered. But it wasn't in her nature to accept defeat without giving it everything she had.

Her grandparents would be back in two short weeks to see how she'd handled her managerial responsibilities. If Holly couldn't figure out a way to make up the income they'd lost, Grandpa might just force her to find a new job. Or worse, demote her. After all the time and hard work she'd put in, being bumped back down to a hand was the worst fate she could imagine.

Knock down cobwebs.

Blitzen gave a bark as he spotted an object behind Holly. She turned to see a red rubber kickball near an old tractor and snowplow before he reached it.

Offer snow-removal services.

She added that one to the brainstorming list, despite how unlikely it was to work. The tractor didn't have a cab, much less a heater. Who on the ranch could she convince to plow driveways with a tractor that sometimes died in the middle of a gravel road? She wasn't even certain it would fire up.

Blitzen pushed the ball with his nose, shoving it in Norbert's direction. The calf, convinced he was really a dog, sprang into action and chased the ball until he too could nudge it with his nose. The two ran alongside, chasing the ball around the open center of the barn.

"Two weeks, guys," Holly said, but her furry friends weren't listening.

"Two weeks?"

Holly jumped at the unexpected voice. *Jillian.* Her eyes widened as she pushed up the sleeve of her sweater to uncover her watch. "I lost track of time."

"How'd I know I'd find you out here?" Her best friend unwrapped the scarf from around her neck, letting it sit loosely on her shoulders. "What's in two weeks?"

"Grandpa and Grandma Charlotte come home."

"That's great, right?"

"I miss them," Holly admitted. Although she had confessed to Jillian that the ranch's financial situation was a little less than spectacular, she hadn't let on how dire it had become. No need to worry anyone else or start rumors circulating about letting people go right before Christmas. "But I'm thinking of ideas to bring in a little more revenue. Grow the business. Make Grandpa proud." Because right now, she felt very much like a failure.

"You had to do that tonight?" Jillian pressed.

Tonight? No. Holly had been desperately trying to come up with a solution for weeks, ever since most of their wheat crop was wiped out by hail. That was before taking the cattle to market at what turned out to be the worst possible time. "Just had a few free minutes."

"You're making a list, huh?" Jillian lifted the notepad off the table and skimmed it.

Holly shrugged. She made lists for just about everything. They kept her organized, sane. "I thought I might at least get it cleaned out. No harm in that."

"And then what?"

That was the million-dollar question. Even if she spent every free minute carrying out the items on that cleaning list, the barn would still stand barren and bring in zero dollars. "Wish I knew." Maybe some grand idea would come to her once it was emptied out.

"I love you, Holl, but nothing on this list will—" Jillian paused midsentence, her eyes stopping on Blitzen and Norbert. "Are they playing *soccer*?"

Holly shrugged, managing to swipe back her notepad. She didn't need the obvious pointed out to her. Every idea on that list was cruddy. "Their version anyway. They have fun with it."

"You sound so nonchalant about this prize-winning video in the making."

To most people, the sight of a fluffy white dog and a medium-sized calf playing together with a rubber ball was a little odd. But Jillian witnessed the event nearly every day. "They're friends."

"I know that." Jillian shook her head. "I just can't

believe they're playing a game together. I've never seen a cow play with a *ball*."

Holly packed up her notepad, pen, and tape measure. "Blitzen taught him."

"Of course he did." Jillian shook her head. "Hey, we have to go. We can't be late tonight. Trish—the *author*—is coming as a guest."

Oh, right. Holly suppressed a groan. Joining the Starlight Book Club had been Jillian's idea. One Holly fought, due to her severe lack of free time and general disinterest in social interaction. "Let me grab my stuff." She turned off the propane heater and reluctantly prepared to abandon the barn.

"You can set aside business for one evening." Jillian patted her shoulder. "I know you're passionate about the ranch, and I adore that about you. But tonight, it's all things Christmas, romance, and peppermint lattes. It's about *relaxing*."

"Well, when you put it that way . . ." Holly didn't want to confess that it'd be impossible to forget about the ranch, even for a couple of hours. Lately, she'd been losing sleep over how to get more money coming in. But for her friend's sake, she'd try to relax a little.

Holly whistled at the animals, and both came barreling toward the door. She let them dart outside into the chilly winter air before cutting the lights.

"You need to record this or something." Jillian nodded toward Blitzen and Norbert. The red rubber ball had found its way outside and was now laying tracks in the fresh dusting of snow as the two continued to play. "Send a video clip in. You might win money!"

"Wouldn't that solve all my problems?" Holly chuckled. *If only.* "I need to grab my book." She hopped up the stairs of the main house. Blitzen abandoned his ball the moment he heard the screen door open, pushing his way around her to dart inside first. Jillian closed the door behind her, leaving Norbert on the front porch to simply stare through the window as Holly had often caught him doing as of late.

"What do you think your grandpa will think of Norbert?"

Holly didn't need to answer the question as she weaved her way through the house to her office. He wouldn't approve, no matter her intentions. But Holly would worry about Norbert later.

The book *Once Upon a Christmas Eve Dance* was buried beneath a hefty pile of papers and ranch ledgers. She made quick work of unearthing it before Jillian could catch her. The truth would likely come out soon enough; she didn't need a lecture already. "Got it," she called.

Blitzen waited in the kitchen doorway for his good-bye treat. Holly dug out a bone-shaped morsel and tossed it to him.

"Ready?" Jillian held out Holly's coat and scarf,

her way of hinting at the time. Holly didn't care to be late, and usually she wasn't, despite something always needing to be done or finished at the worst time. But lately, she'd been stuck in a loop.

"Let's go."

They made it all the way into town and were only two blocks from the downtown strip before Jillian stopped yammering about the book long enough to realize her friend hadn't contributed much to the conversation. "You did *read* it, didn't you?"

Parking, Holly avoided the incredulous stare her best friend sent her from the passenger seat. Instead, she watched snow flurries dust the hood of her truck. "I *meant* to."

"The author will be there!"

"Maybe I can call in sick this time?"

"You're coming in," Jillian insisted. "You made a commitment."

Managing her family's ranch was time-consuming enough. Add to that the ticking clock she was up against, and Holly couldn't have finished a magazine article, let alone an entire book by tonight. "Can you give me the highlights?"

"This isn't like you, Holl."

"Please?"

"I really shouldn't."

Holly wrapped her fuzzy teal scarf around her neck, preparing to face the chilly evening. The Page Turner, a coffee shop slash bookstore, had grown quite popular since it opened its doors almost a year ago. Tonight, they were forced to park a block and a half away. "I don't want to look unprepared. Not in front of the *author*."

"If you had to give a report on cattle prices, you could probably spout that off from memory." Jillian locked eyes with her, and for a moment she worried her best friend wouldn't waver.

"I promise, I'll read the next one."

Jillian pushed her door open and hopped out, forcing Holly to shove the paperback inside her coat and run after her. "It's her Christmas story, Holl. You really didn't even read the first chapter? Skimmed it? Anything?"

"I read the back cover," Holly protested. Truthfully, she attempted to read the back cover three times last night but the words didn't resonate. Too many half-finished lists with weak ideas to generate extra income. Too many worries on her mind.

"It's about a special Christmas Eve ball," Jillian finally said. "This crazy romantic setting—"

"A ball. Christmas. Romantic stuff. Got it."

They hurried along the sidewalk, walking against a light but chilly breeze. Snowflakes caught in her eyelashes. It'd be a pretty sight, if not for the frigid chill in the air. Holly's mind wandered to the calves. With the lowest number the ranch had seen in a decade, their survival of this first winter was crucial.

She'd check on them tonight when they were finished at book club.

"You're thinking about the ranch, aren't you?" Jillian accused as she held the door open.

Holly unwrapped her scarf. "The calves—"

"Brantley is responsible for them, remember?"

Yes, she *did* know that her cousin—Jillian's husband—was tasked with the calves this week. She'd given him the assignment, after all. "But—"

"You trust him, right?"

"I do." Trust had nothing to do with it. Holly had been micromanaging more than ever since their string of bad luck struck.

Jillian tugged on her arm and ushered her over to the group of ladies seated in a circle, most sipping a hot beverage. "Then socialize tonight, Holl. Try enjoying yourself with something completely unrelated to that ranch you're married to." She stopped short of the circle. "Jenny and Pete."

"What?"

"The names of the main characters. You'll need to know that."

That Holly hadn't retained that detail from reading the back cover last night worried her. The author—Trish Meadows—sat in the circle of women talking and smiling. The book cracked open in her lap was one she was signing for someone else. The air felt a little thick. "I shouldn't be here."

"Sit down."

"I need coffee first." Contemplating how she might make the best of this meeting, Holly rushed off to the other side of the bookshop before Jillian could stop her. How could she best avoid the humiliation sure to come when the entire group realized she hadn't read a single page?

Waiting in line to order, Holly discreetly pulled her notepad from her oversized coat pocket. If Jillian spotted it, she'd kill her. She thumbed through the pages until she found the list she left off with, having thought of something to add.

Remove bird nests from rafters.

She wished it was an item that mattered, but it still felt like something.

Lately, she'd been losing sleep. She had nightmares about the ranch heading into foreclosure, all the hands laid off, her grandparents forced to put off retirement. All because she made a few risky decisions that hadn't panned out for the financial future of the ranch.

She'd been as proactive as she was able. The idea to rent out their extra cabins to a couple of writers for the month had been something positive. Though it was a small something in the overall scheme of things, the guests had already paid in full.

That reminded her, she owed her cousin a text. He requested a cabin for a friend of his staying for the holidays. Since they were rented out, she'd have to put him up in the main house. She traded the notepad for her phone and sent off a message to Brantley.

"Mason, your order's ready. Mason."

Holly's head snapped up from her notepad. *Coincidence.* It had to be. There were plenty of other Masons in the world. Surely, even in the small town of Starlight there were a couple.

A tall, broad-shouldered man with a military-precision haircut stepped forward to accept his coffee order. He wasn't in uniform, but he wore combat boots with his jeans. She waited for him to turn around to confirm whether it was really him.

Her stomach flip-flopped in anticipation.

He spun, those steely blue eyes locking with her own.

Mason Montgomery. In the flesh.

Holly froze, choked on words, already embarrassed at what might come out once he said hello. Probably some alien language. She dragged in a deep breath to calm her breathing; it might be the only thing she could control.

Mason nodded at her, then walked away, leaving her standing alone with her mouth agape.

CHAPTER 2

Mason

Mason Montgomery hated traveling during the holidays. Although Christmas was still a few weeks away, the congested airports and delayed flights caused him the same amount of grief. Next time, he'd just drive the entire trip. Better than being routed and rerouted halfway around the country, sometimes in the wrong direction.

He shook away the thought as quickly as it entered. There wouldn't be a next time, because he didn't plan to return to Starlight. He wouldn't be here now if it wasn't a decision forced upon him.

"I want to help you, Montgomery," his commander told him three days earlier. "I want to keep you with us. Got an important mission after Christmas. But first, you need to find a way to resolve this little issue. Get cleared for combat. Go home. You and I both know that's what it's going to take."

Starlight was the only place he'd ever been that truly felt like home.

Before Mason lost both his parents, they'd moved every three to four years. The time he lived here had been with his grandma, who'd been alone for years and unprepared to take in a teenager. But once he started working on the Maxwell Ranch, the family always invited him and his grandma over for holidays. Treated them like part of their family.

He had planned to hunker down at the ranch as soon as possible and lock himself inside the cabin he'd been promised. After too many hours around crowds, he was eager to be settled and away from people. Ready to take the advice he'd been ignoring from his doctor and rest.

But Brantley, his ride and army veteran friend, insisted he wouldn't be able to turn down the allure of Christmas lights lined along Main Street. So Mason begrudgingly gave in to a single trip through the downtown strip to admire decorations and see what had changed over the years he was gone. Then he spotted the coffee shop and asked to stop, because he couldn't fight his craving for a steaming cup. Wyoming winters were just as he remembered: frigid.

"Great coffee," Brantley told him. "Go on, grab a cup. I need to pick up something down the street. Take your time. Meet you back at the truck?"

This new place was a little fancier than he bargained for. Any thought of stealing a few quiet moments by a window and browsing the local newspaper were overruled when he stepped across the threshold and discovered the rows of bookshelves and gaggle of women circling a fireplace. Despite the snowy cold weather, the coffee shop—obviously doubling as a bookstore—bustled with activity.

Too much activity.

He ordered his coffee, met the eyes of the woman behind him in line for a mere second, and rushed out the door, embarrassed by the limp brought on by too much time sitting in a vehicle.

Brantley rambled on about this and that, but Mason hardly heard a word he said. As they traveled over the freshly fallen snow toward the Maxwell Ranch, he couldn't get the woman at the coffee counter out of his head.

Something about her was familiar, but he avoided asking Brantley. Since the insomnia started a couple of months ago, he discovered he couldn't always trust his thoughts. Probably just the curiosity of someone in a small town not recognizing a stranger. For as long as he'd been gone, he might as well be one.

"You promise there aren't any surprise parties or

anything crazy?" Mason couldn't help but ask when he recognized the arch announcing the Maxwell Ranch. The last thing he could bear, outside of a couple of funerals, was an onslaught of people eager to know what he'd been up to the last ten or more years he'd been gone.

"There won't be a soul around tonight."

The house looked the same, despite a black calf standing on the front porch watching him with casual curiosity. The covered porch, the sharply peaked rooflines over the upper windows, even the carved wooden sign displaying the Maxwell family name beside the front door.

Mason dug his duffle bag out of the back seat and set it on the snow-dusted gravel drive as he took it all in.

"Don't mind him," Brantley said once outside the truck. "That's Norbert. He's a bit of a porch ornament."

Mason couldn't imagine Mr. Maxwell approving of livestock roaming freely, but he didn't say that aloud. "Seems a little quiet around here." Although fishing, he hoped he was right. Though Brantley had picked him up from the airport, he granted him the needed silence most of the drive.

"Grandparents have been roaming around the country in an RV all year. They'll be back right around Christmas." He took Mason's duffle bag from him before he could object. It wasn't until Brantley was at the front door that Mason realized something was off.

"I thought I was staying in a cabin?"

"Small mix-up, I'm afraid. Cabins are all full. But we have a room for you in the house."

Mason's throat constricted. Stay in a house filled with people? He couldn't possibly do that. The last thing he wanted was anyone worrying about him for any reason. He had no intention of mentioning his insomnia or the order he had to come home. "I was hoping for somewhere quiet." He hoped Brantley, having served time with him, would've understood that.

"I promise, this room is as quiet as you'll get in a cabin." Brantley led them inside.

"How are things with the ranch?" he asked, desperate to distract himself from the panic creeping its way in. As promised, the house was empty. Not a soul around. *Odd.* The house had always bustled with half a dozen people or more. "Do you live here now?" Spotting the gold band on his finger, he added, "With your wife?"

"Oh, no." Brantley shook his head and led Mason through the living room, its tall windows overlooking the peaceful, familiar backyard. He'd spent a few holidays with the Maxwells in this room, comfortable on a section of couch watching football or whatever Christmas movie was playing on TV. "Jillian and I have our own cabin on the other side of the ranch. One I built myself a few years back."

He recalled Brantley had always been quite handy, but building an entire cabin was quite impressive. He couldn't imagine Paul even knowing where to start on such a project.

Gut-wrenching sadness hit him like a boulder to the stomach, but he fought to keep his expression neutral. Blank. Paul, Brantley's late brother and Mason's best friend, had been killed in combat more than three years ago. This place would never be the same without him wandering around, tinkering with a camera or bragging about some computer he built himself.

"Holly does, though."

"Holly?"

"Yeah. She's the last of us cousins who does."

Mason had to sift through his memories, unreliable of late, but the name did sound familiar. He was having trouble placing her. "Holly?"

"You remember, I'm sure. Always out there working with us? Always trying to prove she could do anything we could."

"Oh, Holly." Mason remembered the kid in pigtails and a cowgirl hat a size or two too big, eager to be in the middle of everything. Never afraid to get her hands dirty. She could ride a horse to move cattle with the best of them. "She stays here now?"

"She *runs* things now."

"As in manages?"

"Yep." Brantley waved him up a spiral staircase in the back of the house. Mason had never been up the stairs, but he remembered seeing them often and wondering. "It's a private suite, separate from the rest of the second floor."

Perfect.

Brantley pushed open the door and allowed him to step inside. His eyes traveled immediately to a pile of white fur curled up on the bed. The dog lifted his head groggily at the sight of visitors, his tail wagging against the comforter.

"This is Blitzen."

"Does he come with the room?" Mason dropped his smaller bag and approached the dog with caution, though Blitzen looked about as ferocious as a sugar cookie. The dog licked his hand and eagerly accepted the rubs he offered.

"Holly's dog. Not sure how he got up here."

"I don't mind." It'd been a long time since he was around a dog. He kept busy, worked later than most soldiers, volunteered for any deployment he could. Having a dog had never been something he could justify.

"There's a tuft box in the closet. Belongs to you. Mom left it with me when she moved."

"Thanks." He'd left a few things behind when he joined the army. Definitely a pair of cowboy boots. He wasn't sure what else after all this time. Probably a bunch of clothes that no longer fit and trinkets he didn't need. "I might rest a bit, if you don't mind?"

"Sure thing." Door halfway closed, Brantley added, "My mom moved to Arizona a couple of years ago, but she'll be coming back in a few days for the holidays. Staying here too, just so you're aware. I know she's looking forward to seeing you."

Mason gave him a nod. Amelia West had been like a second mother to him after losing both his parents. He'd be glad to see her. Hopefully, she wasn't as perceptive as he remembered, or the real reason he finally accepted the Maxwell's holiday invitation would be out in the open in no time.

Mason sat down on the bed next to Blitzen. "So, you're Holly's dog, huh?" When the white golden retriever rolled onto his back and pinned him with large, pitiful eyes, Mason couldn't deny the pup a good belly rub. He wished more than anything he could lay down on the bed, shut his eyes, and drift off into a peaceful sleep. The jackpot would be if he could sleep solid until the next morning.

But weeks had gone by since he was lucky enough to sleep more than two hours at a time. And never without that dull shooting pain in his leg that came with nightmares of the ambush.

CHAPTER 3

Holly

Peppermint latte in hand, Holly forced herself to rejoin the book club near the fireplace. She still couldn't shake the interaction with Mason. Did he not recognize her? It *had* been almost a decade since he was last in Starlight. But with all the time she spent working alongside him as a teenager, she'd at least expected a friendly hello.

"That took long enough." Jillian eyed her suspiciously, making Holly wonder if she witnessed the incident, however brief.

"Long line."

Unbuttoning her coat, Holly hung it over the back of the chair Jillian had saved for her. Maybe her disappointment in Mason not recognizing her had more to do with that embarrassing schoolgirl crush she had on him than anything. She'd spent a lot of time daydreaming about him back then.

"Sure." Jillian wasn't buying her excuse.

Holly recognized some of the members, like Lina Holbrook, another ranch owner. Trish was her future granddaughter-in-law. And there was Abbie Bennington, from the *Starlight Gazette*. Holly couldn't remember whether she was a member or joining the group to write an article.

Others were unfamiliar, but she recognized enough of the ladies to feel inadequate. What would they think if they realized Holly hadn't even *started* the book? She dug the paperback out of her coat pocket and discreetly turned it over so she could once again read the back cover. Maybe she could sneak in the first couple of pages if she was sly enough.

"This might be about everyone for tonight," Mitzy Collins, the head of the book club, announced. The weather, she informed everyone, had kept a couple members at home. Their little town didn't see much snowfall in the winter, but tonight the heavy flakes were accumulating quickly. Another reason Holly felt compelled to get back to the ranch as soon as possible.

The group chattered about the weather forecast for a good ten minutes, buying Holly enough time to skim the first three pages. But try as she may, she was too distracted by not only ranch issues, but by bumping into Mason, too.

"Brantley has everything under control," Jillian assured her. "You have to trust him. Like your grandpa trusts you."

"Okay." Though in a few weeks, her grandpa wouldn't trust her to move a herd, much less manage a ranch. "But if the weather gets any worse, we have to go or we might get stranded in town."

The thought of being stranded and poor Norbert not able to sneak into the back porch to sleep if snow drifted over the doggie door tore at her. Blitzen would throw a fit if that happened. Maybe she treated Norbert more like a dog than she should, but he'd barely survived the spring. It was a miracle he was still with them.

"I have a list of discussion questions," Mitzy announced, interrupting the weather chatter and bringing their focus back to the book. "Let's start with the first one: Do you think the story was character driven or plot based?"

Holly swallowed and ducked her head. Why couldn't the first question be an easy one? She could fake her way through liking a character. Her usual ability to make the best of a bad situation seemed to be failing her tonight.

"Character driven." Jillian spoke up right away. "The choices Jenny makes throughout the story are what drives everything that happens. It's her quirky, impulsive personality that sets everything in motion," Jillian went on, making Holly feel smaller and smaller with each additional thought. Smaller yet when others chimed in. It wasn't like her not to do her homework for something like this, and she didn't care for the unpreparedness she felt.

"Without Jenny, that gala would *never* have turned out like it did," another said.

"There wouldn't have even *been* a gala!" said Mitzy. "And that's the best part of the whole story."

Holly pried open the front cover and tried again to read the first page, hoping for some revelation there so she could contribute to the group. But her attempt to sneak-read backfired when her notepad plopped to the floor.

"You brought your *notebook*?" Jillian asked through gritted teeth.

"To take notes."

"Liar."

Adverse to relying on technology, Holly hardly went anywhere without a notepad of some kind. Her mind was always spinning with to-dos, and she didn't want to miss a single one if she was unable to jot it down. "I might need it," she defended.

"Oh, I loved the barn!" Lina clapped her hands together.

Holly's attention averted back to the conversation, wondering what she missed during the brief argument.

"That was my favorite theme! How they kept coming back to it," another said. "Such a romantic setting for a Christmas gala, don't you think?"

"Perfect, actually," Holly said before anyone could steal her chance to contribute *something* to the conversation, because now she felt she finally could. "When I was a little girl, I used to pretend the old barn on our property was a grand ballroom in some lavish hotel or castle. I'd spin around in circles until I got dizzy and fell into a pile of hay."

"That's adorable!" Abbie said.

"A rustic barn would be so fun to fix up," Mitzy added. "Could you imagine?"

"I have a small confession." Trish's cheeks turned an adorably light shade of pink. "Ever since I was a little girl, I've secretly wanted to organize a Christmas Eve dance in an old barn. The story, well, all the details of that barn and the dance are just like I've always imagined them. Down to the white Christmas lights wrapped around the rafters, the excessive number of Christmas trees, and mistletoe everywhere!"

"How fun!" one said.

"You should do it!" Mitzy this time, her eyes sparkling with excitement at the very idea. "It would be so perfect to recreate a gala just like the one you gave Jenny and Pete." Three women—maybe four—shared a collective blissful sigh.

"It would be fun, wouldn't it?" Trish admitted, but her smile quickly faded. "I'll be honest, I've looked around. Mostly when I should've been writing my next book." A few chuckles sounded at that. "But I haven't found anything like that barn. Not near Starlight, and well, I just couldn't dream of having one anywhere else."

Mitzy turned her attention to Holly, and for a moment, heat rushed to her cheeks. Had she been caught sneak-reading? "You have a barn."

"I wasn't— I mean I— *What?*"

A twinkle danced across Lina's eyes. "You do."

"Well, it's a work in progress at the moment," she said. The amount of effort it would take to get it ready for something as lavish as a gala would be astronomical. She couldn't afford to hire anyone, and the hands were busy enough right now. "Not exactly ready for a Christmas ball."

"That's a shame," Trish said, the excitement fading from her expression.

But she *could* clean it out. Decorate it.

"Yeah, that is too bad," Mitzy agreed. "I bet we'd sell out in two days flat."

Tickets? The wheels spun through her mind. If something like this sold *tickets,* it would mean a venue rental fee. A sizable one for an event that large. "I could get it ready," Holly heard herself say before she could stop herself. "It's not being used for anything else."

"Think it would be for Christmas Eve?" Lina asked, hope in those happy eyes. "Trish and I can take care of the setup."

"I have decorations I could donate. An extra tree you could borrow," Abbie chimed in.

"Me, too," Mitzy offered. A few others did as well.

Trish slipped Holly a piece of paper. "Would that cover a reservation?"

One thousand dollars! Holly calculated the days between now and Christmas Eve in her head, wondering how much sleep she would have to sacrifice to make it happen. Plus the heating costs . . . Could they stay under budget with upkeep and repairs and turn a profit? Because without a profit, Grandpa would surely flip.

"All that hard work could pay off in the future," Lina added. "I have a great-niece looking for a spring wedding venue. She's set on a barn."

"Yes, it can be ready by then." She wished she felt the confidence she portrayed in her tone. Because this *had* to work. Converting the barn into a venue might be a steady revenue stream in the future.

"This Christmas Eve. So exciting!" Mitzy clapped her hands together and let out a tiny squeal of excitement. "Can we come see the barn?"

"Uh—" Holly felt the pressure mount as everyone leaned forward in their chairs, eagerly awaiting her answer. How could she tell a group of excited, hopeful women no? "Give me a few days to get it cleaned up a bit."

"Of course!"

It might take a Christmas miracle to pull this off, but if she could, maybe her grandpa would decide she wasn't a complete failure after all.

Mitzy clapped her hands again, this time to rein everyone back in to their main purpose. "Let's talk about Pete and his snowman tree!"

That none of the members called her out for not reading the book left her relieved and grateful for the free pass.

"Are you nuts?" Jillian smacked Holly with her paperback once they were outside the bookstore, heading back toward the truck.

"Okay, so maybe it's a *little* rash."

"Holly, you're not the rash one. *I* am."

They both let out a laugh at that, because it was true. Holly was normally levelheaded. Had the cattle gotten a decent price at market or the wheat crop not been obliterated by a storm, she might've exercised the good sense to at least tell the group she'd get back to them. *After* she ran the numbers and calculated the realistic hours needed to pull it all off.

"Did you see them in there?" Holly unlocked the truck but took her time unwrapping her scarf before she opened her door and climbed in. She needed a moment to collect herself so Jillian wouldn't sense her panic or the pressure. "Everyone seemed so excited about the idea. I couldn't crush their hopes and dreams."

"Is that what you're going to tell your grandpa?"

"It's an opportunity to grow the ranch. As a *business*." Grandpa often asked Holly what she was doing to grow her business, to put her in the mindset of a business owner. It was something he'd asked her since she was a young teenager. She left out the detail that the ranch needed money or that she would keep this under wraps until he came home. "Hoping he'll give me points for creativity." She tried to laugh, but it came out weak.

"You're really going through with this?"

"Yes."

"But you didn't even read the book!"

"I will." She wasn't sure when, but she'd make the time. Volunteering allowed her to avoid questions about the novel she didn't read, but she'd make it right when she found some spare time.

"You can't recreate something you know nothing about."

At a stop sign, Holly turned to face her friend. "Maybe you could help me out?"

"What if you *do* pull this off?" Jillian asked. "Then what?"

It was a risk, Holly knew that. "This could give the ranch options. I want us to keep the herd if market prices are grim." She never again wanted the decision to be dictated by the need to keep the ranch running. Payrolls fulfilled. "What if we could guarantee that income without relying on market prices or unpredictable weather?" If she could pull this off, Holly might open an entirely new revenue stream for the future.

"What are you saying?"

What *was* she saying? She wasn't quite sure. "Maybe the barn could become an actual venue, as Lina suggested." The idea might be a little farfetched. Turning it into a winter wonderland, even for an evening, required a substantial amount of work. If it was a successful event, nothing guaranteed they'd ever book another.

"For weddings and events?" Jillian offered.

"Why not?" She wanted to believe in the idea. Needed to believe in it. Because when her grandpa flipped out at this latest project the ranch couldn't afford, it would be her only line of defense.

CHAPTER 4

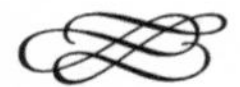

Mason

Mason never had been good at sitting still, even before the bouts of insomnia. After Brantley left him alone in his room, he unpacked his duffle into the dresser drawers. Anything to work out the stiffness in that leg. He rolled up T-shirts and socks in tight, orderly fashion. Folded jeans meticulously.

Blitzen watched him from the comfort of the bed, intrigued but much too comfortable to hop down.

Next, he sifted quickly through the tote Brantley mentioned, long enough to recover the pair of cowboy boots. It'd been almost a decade since he last put them on, and he was surprised to find they still fit comfortably.

Without more to do in the lonely bedroom, he ventured into the kitchen. This time, the dog followed. But Mason found the fridge nearly bare. He grabbed his coat and headed outside.

He shoveled the freshly fallen snow off the porch steps and from the winding sidewalk, the black calf following him curiously as Blitzen watched from the window. The dog dozed lazily in and out of sleep on an ottoman pushed up against the glass.

Mason was just putting the shovel back in the shed near the main house when headlights lit up the driveway. Holly, he suspected.

Despite his best attempts, he just couldn't picture the kid in pigtails all grown up and managing the entire ranch. He shouldn't be surprised, though; Holly being Lawrence Maxwell's granddaughter, the woman was probably tough as nails. Mr. Maxwell was a very smart businessman and would never leave someone in charge he wasn't completely confident in.

"Hello," came the hesitant greeting. The headlight beams still shone in his eyes, and he couldn't quite make her out.

"Holly?" he asked.

"Yes. What are *you* doing here?"

He shoved his hands in his pockets as awkwardness danced between them. If he hadn't already called the hotel in town to learn they were booked solid, he'd find a way there now. As it was, he planned to call and see if they had any cancellations. He hated the thought of inconveniencing the family that had been so good to him all those years ago. "Did Brantley not mention I was staying here?"

"Ah, *you're* the one?" Headlights blinked off, and the glow of the porchlight exposed the pink in her cheeks, contrasted against dark curls. "I should've known."

"Let's head inside," he said. "It's too cold out to be standing around talking."

For a moment, he thought she'd argue. But within seconds, her feet skittered up the freshly shoveled stairs to the front door. "Thanks for clearing the sidewalk," she said before disappearing inside.

He took his time, kicking the snow off his boots on the porch. The woman he just watched walk past him couldn't possibly be the kid who used to tag along with them, determined to work as hard as *the boys*.

Inside, he found her still in coat and scarf, lying on the large ottoman. She had Blitzen wrapped in her arms. His tail wagged in double time, and he snuck in a lick to her cheek. "I missed you too, buddy. Hope you were good to our guest."

"He was."

Holly rolled off the ottoman and hopped to her feet. She busied herself with unwrapping her scarf and looking anywhere but at him. He should look away, but he was trying to place the girl from his memory. The woman standing before him mesmerized him . . . those dark curls and darker eyes. Then it hit him and Mason looked away. "You were at the coffee shop."

"Yep, that was me."

"I'm sorry," he apologized, and he meant it. "It's been so long. I didn't recognize—"

"Not a problem." She hung her scarf and coat on a hook near the front door. "So, Brantley set you up with the second-floor suite in the back, I assume?"

"If staying here is a problem—"

"No, it's fine." Holly slipped off her boots, revealing red socks with some green decoration. Ornaments maybe? Or possibly Christmas lights? "I overbooked the cabins. Definitely my fault you didn't have a place to stay. Forgot Brantley asked until he reminded me last night."

"You're sure it's okay?"

"Yes, yes." Holly waved him toward the kitchen with the book in her hand, Blitzen already beating both of them there. "You want a cup of coffee? If you're worried about the caffeine, I can make decaf."

If only it were as simple as cutting out caffeine, but Mason wouldn't let on to any of that. No one, especially Holly Maxwell, needed to know about his trouble sleeping. Maybe a few days on the ranch would revive him and he'd find himself cured and out cold through the night again. "Coffee sounds great. I'll take whatever you make."

She directed him to a barstool on the opposite side of the breakfast island, leaving the paperback cover down on the granite. His back faced the big kitchen window, but he tried not to let that bother him. He reassured himself that the only threat behind him might be a curious peeping cow.

"How long you sticking around?"

Strange how Holly couldn't look him in the eyes. He wondered if he'd offended her somehow. Maybe it was simply a matter of inconveniencing her. She had a quiet house all to herself until he arrived.

"Maybe a week or two. Haven't really decided." His commander didn't expect him back until the end of the month, but Mason wasn't sure he could handle being so far away from his duties for that long. Even if he was stuck at the base and it was quieter this time of year, there was still work to be done. And once he was cleared for duty, reenlistment paperwork to sign. Deployment orders to track down.

"You don't want to go back before Christmas, do you?" She fished a dog treat out of the cupboard and tossed it to Blitzen.

Truthfully, he wanted to go back right now. He didn't like sitting idle in this kitchen in Wyoming when there were good men and women overseas facing grave danger every minute. He wanted to be there, fighting alongside them. The army, it was all he knew. But he was one signature shy of returning to the action. "We'll see."

Back still turned toward him as she busied herself with mugs, Holly said, "Grandpa and Grandma Charlotte won't be home for two weeks. You should at least stick around until they get back. I know they'd love seeing you."

Mason hoped to get a handle on his sleepless nights as quickly as possible. Two weeks felt like an eternity. If he could return to duty next week, he'd leave the instant he knew he'd be cleared. "I don't know that I could keep myself occupied for that long."

"You never were good at sitting still, were you?"

It surprised him that she remembered that detail. It had to have been ten years or more since he last worked on the ranch. With the number of other ranch hands, it surprised him that he stood out in her memory at all. She'd always been sharp, though; he remembered that about her. "I like to keep busy, yes." Mason had hoped to help around the ranch to fill his time, and asked Holly, "You need any extra hands?"

She poured him a cup and slid it across the counter without offering extras. "We're actually staffed just right."

He struggled to withhold a scowl. Holly wasn't responsible for his disappointment. He couldn't sit in the house all day, though. He'd lose his mind. Maybe he could find temporary work on another ranch. He worked at a few off and on during his teen years. Surely someone would accept free help over the holidays. Anything to remain busy and keep his leg moving. If he was active, it wasn't hurting.

Blitzen nudged his arm with a wet nose, demanding more rubs. Mason obliged, then took a cautious sip. *Hint of peppermint?* It'd been a long time since he had a cup this good. Mr. Maxwell had never scrimped on the quality of his coffee. He'd always been a generous man when it came to sharing thermoses of it with his hands, too.

"I do have a project I could use help with, though. If you're interested."

"What's that?"

"I need to fix up the old red barn. You remember, the one we used to keep the hay in? It needs to be cleaned out. Spruced up a bit. That sort of thing."

Something in her offer gave him the distinct impression she was leaving something out, but he didn't pry. Manual labor, it sounded like the perfect thing to keep him occupied. And if he recalled the right barn, the size of it promised plenty. "The old red one, on the south end?"

"Yeah, that one."

"You don't use it anymore?"

Holly carried her own mug to the counter, joining him. After a sip, she set it down and leaned her arms against the granite. "There's a new barn now that we keep most of the hay in. This old one has some of the extra, but we can move it." Something flashed in those dark eyes. Concern? Doubt? Mason wasn't sure.

"Got big plans for Ol' Red?"

"Something like that." She was back to not meeting his eyes, and he wanted to know what she wasn't telling him. But after all this time, after skipping out on all the previous holiday invitations he'd received from the Maxwells, he didn't feel he had the right to pry.

Instead, he asked, "What do you need me to do?"

"Help clean it out, for starters." She pulled a notepad from beneath the paperback, flipped a few pages in, and slid it across the counter.

"A list."

"A long one. But you said you wanted something to do."

"I do."

"I have to warn you, it doesn't pay much."

Mason skimmed the items, undaunted by any of the tasks. A lot of manual labor involved, but that was his favorite kind. "I don't want money." The family was already offering him a free place to stay, and would no doubt go out of their way to ensure his comfort. He couldn't fathom accepting a dime he didn't need anyway.

She flashed him a challenging smile. "If you want me to try to change your mind on that, you're negotiating with the wrong girl."

Girl was hardly the term. "I'm not here to make money."

Blitzen suddenly dashed to the window, causing both Mason and Holly to watch with curiosity.

"Norbert."

"The cow?"

Holly shrugged. "They're besties."

Mason raised an eyebrow at that, but she didn't elaborate. Instead, she studied him a moment. The longest moment she'd let her eyes stay on him rather than skitter away. "Why *are* you here?"

The blunt questions shouldn't surprise him. She'd always asked those. But he seemed choked for words without an answer he could easily provide. Mason suspected Holly would discover his lie if he tried to tell one. "When can I start on the barn?"

She let out a dissatisfied sigh but let her question go unanswered. "I have a few things to take care of in the morning. I can take you out there tomorrow afternoon. Say two?"

Mason sucked in a breath and hid his disapproval with his coffee mug, taking a slow sip. Panic tried its best to ball up in his chest, and he wondered what he could possibly do to fill his time before Holly showed him the barn. "Anything else you'd like done in the meantime?" he finally asked.

"Nope. Just relax. You have to be jetlagged, right?" She fidgeted with the paperback on the counter, keeping the title hidden from him. Was she embarrassed at what she was reading?

"What's that?"

Pink rushed to her cheeks, and she pushed it aside. Leaning against the counter again, she let her arms hide it. "Nothing. Just a book we read for our book club meeting."

"Any good?"

"Oh yeah, wonderful story! The author lives here in town."

"Maybe I could read it, then?" He had discovered reading brought him a little bit of comfort late into most sleepless nights. The reading itself never made him tired, but it did help pass the time and take his mind off the aching pain in his leg.

"Oh, I don't think you'd like it. It's really girly."

"Try me."

Holly bit her bottom lip, and he found the expression quite adorable. "It's a romance novel."

Not his preference, at all. But tonight, he wouldn't argue with *any* reading material. He'd looked through the nightstand drawers in his room, but there wasn't even an outdated magazine. "I'm always open to trying something new."

"I kind of need this book for something I'm working on."

"I'm a fast reader."

Holly started some further rebuttal, but was left with her mouth agape. A few seconds passed before she huffed out a laugh. "You really are relentless, aren't you?" Something playful danced in her eyes. No way she was *flirting* with him. He shook the thought as soon as it entered. He could never think of her in that way. The Maxwells were his second family. Lawrence had never been shy about reminding his hired help that his granddaughters were off limits. Best to rid of that thought before it ever had time to take root.

"Just forgot to pack reading material, that's all."

"Oh, well, if that's all." Holly pushed up from the counter, emptied what was left in her mug into the sink and rinsed it. "There're a couple of bookshelves in the office. Kind of a random mishmash of books, but you're guaranteed to find something more to your liking than this."

Mason emptied his cup and followed Holly. Blitzen, torn between abandoning his buddy at the window and getting left behind, whimpered. "Just a minute, Blitz. We'll get Norbert settled in after I find our guest a good book."

"Settled in?"

She wouldn't meet his eyes again. "Norbert likes to sleep on the back porch."

"I might just have to stay until Christmas," Mason said. "I'm curious to meet this new grandpa of yours who allows livestock to roam free and sleep inside." He meant it as a joke, but those cheeks turned pink again.

"He doesn't know." Holly reached around a door jamb, flipping on a light in the darkened room. "Books are over there, against that wall." She pointed. "I need to get Norbert settled in or Blitzen will have a small meltdown. He's still getting used to the doggie dog."

She slipped out of the room before Mason could question the odd situation further, leaving him alone with a bunch of books and his thoughts. But his eyes wandered to the massive oak desk in the middle of the room, covered with ledgers and notepads. Crumpled notebook pages were scattered on top, and a few had dropped onto the floor.

Hearing the creak of the back door, Mason allowed himself to approach the desk. Seemed Holly hadn't quite inherited her grandpa's knack for tidiness. But he had no doubt those ledgers were perfectly done, the calculations and projections correct.

It reminded him of the time Lawrence offered him a permanent job. One with the potential to be groomed to manage a ranch someday. Instead of taking him up on the offer, he joined the army as he'd always planned. And Paul followed.

He briefly wondered how different his life would be if he hadn't made that one critical decision, but the *what if* fled quickly. Though he had enjoyed working on a ranch—the reward of a hard day's work and the peaceful environment—he knew from a young age that he would follow in his parents' bootsteps.

The creaking of hardwood warned him Holly was nearby. He quickly abandoned his fascination with the array of wadded papers on the desk and pulled the first book he could reach off the shelf.

"You find something?"

"Yep." He tucked the book under his arm.

"You eaten? I can't offer much more than a PB and J right now . . ."

He hadn't, but he wasn't hungry. His stomach would no doubt take a couple of days to untangle from its knots. Being back here, it brought back a lot of memories. Memories he was trying hard to suppress. He couldn't change the past, so why live there? "I think I'll head to bed if that's okay. Jetlag and all."

Her smile dimmed, and something he couldn't explain tugged at him. "Of course."

"Thank you for putting me up." Blitzen trotted into the office, sitting at Holly's feet and leaning in until she scratched behind his ears.

"You're always welcome to stay here, Mason."

"Goodnight, Holly."

CHAPTER 5

Sleep had all but eluded Holly. Mason Montgomery was sleeping in *her* house. He might have been on the complete opposite end of the house and on a whole different floor, but it didn't change the fact the guy she spent her teenage years crushing hard on was staying with them, possibly through Christmas.

"You're blushing." Jillian pointed a half-eaten glazed donut at her from the opposite side of the kitchen island. "Why are you blushing?"

Holly scanned the room and surrounding areas. She hoped Blitzen would alert her to Mason if he appeared, but the dog was pretty fixated on the donuts Bobby, one of her cousins and ranch hands, had picked up from Millie's Bakery at her request. "Two words: Mason Montgomery."

Jillian dropped her donut, Blitzen intently watching. "As in *the* Mason? I get the special donut run now."

"Apparently *your husband* invited him to stay with us for the holidays." Holly stared her friend down, determined to learn whether Jillian had any insight. "You didn't happen to forget to mention something to me, did you?"

"Of course not! Brantley said it was an old army buddy. He didn't tell me it was *Mason*." Jillian hopped off her stool, donut recovered, and paced around the kitchen, craning her head through doorways. "Where is he?"

"Knock that off. He's still asleep."

"It's almost nine. Isn't he in the army? You know, used to early mornings and all that?"

Holly pulled apart her ring-shaped donut and tossed a piece to a very eager Blitzen. He gobbled it up whole and stood at attention, ready for more should it come. "He spent the day traveling. I think." She realized she never asked *where* he was coming from. It was crazy enough to think they stood in the kitchen last night and had an adult conversation.

For months after he left, Holly missed him terribly. Dreamed about him coming back and saying he couldn't bear to be away from her anymore. But she'd been a careless teenager pining after someone who didn't even know she existed. Now that she was an adult and managing a ranch, she wasn't suspectable to such foolish notions.

"Is he still cute?" Jillian asked, returning to the island.

"What?"

"Oh, come on, now. Stop playing dumb. Answer the question."

"In that dashing, serious military kind of way, sure." It was an understatement, and they both knew it. "I'm not some teenage girl anymore, you know. Haven't even thought about him in years. I've moved on."

Jillian laughed. "Oh, really?"

"Really."

"And *who* have you moved on to?" Challenge danced in Jillian's eyes, daring Holly to answer. "I can't even remember the last time you went on a date."

"I've been busy managing a ranch, thank you." Plus, their small town didn't offer many prospects who appealed to her. She'd grown up with so many of them and could hardly imagine herself dating anyone here. She'd tried, but Jillian was right. It'd been quite a while since her last failed attempt.

"There're a few cute ranch hands who work for you."

"Exactly. They *work* for me," Holly said. "That makes them off limits."

"Says who?"

Holly closed the donut box and slid it to the side. She'd requested extra for Mason. The man had to be starving. It wasn't the most nutritious breakfast, but her bare cupboards didn't promise much else. "I don't date anyone who works on the ranch. You know that."

"Mason doesn't work for you. You could date him."

At that comment, Holly shot a panicked glance around the room. The last thing she needed was an embarrassing episode in which Mason Montgomery overheard this conversation. She'd never confessed her feelings, and if she went the rest of her life without Mason knowing of the terrible crush she had on him when she was fourteen, that would be okay with her.

"Actually, as of today he *does* work for me. He's going to help clean out the barn." That he wasn't on the payroll was a detail Holly didn't care to offer up to her friend. The fewer loopholes offered to Jillian's devious mind, the better. "And he's still in the army, in case you missed that detail."

"So?"

"So, it means he leaves in a couple of weeks. It might be another decade before he comes back to Starlight." Holly retrieved a treat for Blitzen then forced Jillian to follow her to the front door or be left behind. "I'm done talking about this."

Holly didn't wait for Jillian to catch up before she headed straight for the truck. She still hadn't decided whether having Mason on the ranch for the holidays was a good thing or not. But the free help he offered couldn't have been better timed.

"What are we doing again?" Jillian asked in the truck.

"I need to get some cleaning supplies for the barn." She had spent the better part of her morning rounding up what she could from around the ranch—old brooms, both for sweeping and knocking down cobwebs; a shop vac she hoped would run until they didn't need it anymore; enough old rags to cover the barn floor. But she was short several items, much to her dismay. "You don't have to go with me if you have appointments."

"Nothing until this afternoon, for a change." Jillian fastened her seat belt, holding on to the strap as she turned to Holly. "You're just going to leave Mason home alone?"

"He's Brantley's guest, remember?" Before Jillian had a chance to retort, Holly changed the subject. "I need to make a list of everything we'll need to recreate the barn from Trish's story. Can you help me with that?" She'd made a cleaning list and a preliminary list of decorations that included the trees, white lights, and snowman collection the ladies mentioned at book club last night. But the rest was a mystery to her.

"Holl, you *still* haven't read the book?"

"No, I didn't manage to read the entire book last night." She hadn't cracked it open even, but Jillian didn't need to know that. She'd been much too distracted by the memories that played over and over in her mind—of Mason working on the ranch—to do anything as involved as reading a book.

"If you want my help, you have to read it."

The couple of inches of snow that fell last night coated fields and dusted tree branches. With the sun glistening off the white crystals, the winter landscape reminded Holly of a painting. Outside of the challenge of keeping livestock alive during the severely cold temperatures, she really did love this time of year.

"I *will* read it," Holly finally said, at the edge of the ranch before they rolled onto the gravel road to town. "Starting tonight."

"At least a chapter a day."

"Fine." Holly was certain she could fit one tiny chapter somewhere into her day. She had quite enjoyed reading at one time, which was the reason Jillian talked her into a book club to begin with. But over the past couple of years, she hadn't had time to finish a single novel. A chapter a night, though it felt impossible to squeeze in, might be a nice, temporary escape from the reality that the ranch hadn't performed well under her management. The dread, well . . . she didn't like to think about it.

"Two would be better."

"Don't press your luck."

"I want a report each morning on the chapter you read."

Holly let out a defeated sigh. "Is that the only way you'll agree to help me?"

"Yes."

"Done." The edge of Starlight appeared at the base of the hill they crested, a sight that always made her smile. She'd been born and raised in this little Wyoming town and couldn't imagine living anywhere else. Starlight was home.

Hopefully her grandpa wouldn't fire her. If he did, she might be forced to move somewhere no one had ever heard of her. No one in town would even want her mucking out their stables if Lawrence Maxwell deemed her unfit to run a ranch.

"I'll put something together to help get you started, but lists are your thing."

"Thank you." Parked in front of the local hardware store, Holly flipped through her notebook once more. "How many people do you think we should plan for?" That detail had escaped her last night when she was drafting a profit and loss for the event.

Jillian shrugged. "Maybe seventy-five? I don't really know. Suppose it depends how many people the book club gets jazzed up about it. Aren't tickets and all that Trish's area?"

"Yeah." Thankfully. Holly was definitely *not* an

event planner. "They should take care of flyers and all that too, right?" Marketing had never been a particularly strong suit of hers, and in the ranching business, it wasn't entirely necessary. The Maxwell cattle had always maintained their own reputation simply by word of mouth. But without proper advertising, this entire Christmas Eve gala would be a bust.

"Lina already had one drafted. Didn't she send you a copy? She emailed one out to the book club."

"Guess I missed that email." Holly shook her head. "At least that means I only need to worry about a few trees and some lights."

Jillian shook her head in disbelief. "You really need to read that book."

Holly fought an annoying pitter-patter in her chest as she led Mason to the barn on the south end of the property. Blitzen and Norbert ran alongside them, red ball rolling in the barn's general direction. She wondered what Mason must think of something she'd become so accustomed to.

"So you stayed?" he asked. "Here in Starlight?"

Why did it feel as if she were fourteen again? Holly closed her eyes, took a deep breath, and reminded herself they were adults now. The ridiculous schoolgirl crush was a thing of the past, and

Mason would leave again. Most importantly, family friend or not, he worked for her now. "Went to college, but I came back after that and stayed on."

"To manage the ranch?"

Holly shrugged. "Yeah, that was always my plan."

"Really." Mason sounded . . . intrigued. She'd been mocked by more than a few men, mostly on those horrific dates, for wanting such a thing out of life. "I admire that."

"You do?"

"You had a plan. You stuck to it, made it happen."

She flashed him a smile, but turned away before it weakened into a frown. Since a young age, she had always planned to someday run the Maxwell Ranch. Everything she did, the questions she annoyed people with growing up, they were all for a purpose. But if she didn't find a way to turn that red number into a fat, healthy green one soon, she wouldn't be managing anything.

"You stayed in the army."

"Yes."

Blitzen zipped in front of them to retrieve the ball that had shot off into a line of trees. "Is that your calling?"

Mason's face blanked. "Calling. That's a strong word. I wouldn't say that. But it does give me purpose."

Something about his answer felt riddled with unknowns, but she wasn't sure how to ask about that. Instead, she stepped over a fallen branch coated in a dusting of snow and asked, "You're staying in a while, then?"

"Yeah. A lifer, as they call it."

It shouldn't disappoint her, but the declaration did. It meant Mason would most definitely leave, and he may not come back. She was still trying to figure out what had driven him to come this year after more than a decade of declined invitations.

"Where you at these days anyway?"

"Fort Bragg."

Holly thought a moment, but the name of the base didn't help her place it on a map. "Where's that?"

"North Carolina."

A silly part of Holly's heart sank. North Carolina. On the complete opposite side of the country. Of course he was. "You like it there?"

He shrugged, his eyes locked straight ahead. "It's not a bad place."

"Do you miss Starlight?" She shouldn't care so much about his answer, but she caught herself holding her breath. No matter what he said, it wouldn't change anything between them. There wasn't even a *them* to consider.

"Not really."

"Oh."

"I've spent my entire life traveling from place to place. Hard to miss places when you know you won't stay anywhere for long."

Holly couldn't relate. She'd only ever left Starlight to attend college. She'd missed it terribly the entire time she was gone. She tried to imagine what it must be like to never call anywhere home. "Do you think you'll ever settle down in one place?" She wasn't asking because she'd been fantasizing about them getting married and running a ranch together. Definitely not.

Mason kicked at the ball in his path, sending both Norbert and Blitzen in a race after it a few dozen yards ahead. "I don't stay still very well."

CHAPTER 6

Mason

The trip to the old barn required some trudging through the snow, but Norbert and Blitzen raced ahead and cleared a path through the fresh inches of powder. "They're quite a pair, those two." Mason still couldn't get past the young cow roaming free on a ranch that'd been run so strictly.

"Norbert almost didn't make it through the spring." Holly kept pace without any indication they were moving too quickly. He slowed his brisk stride anyway. They weren't marching to a field exercise, after all. "His mother wouldn't claim him, no matter what we tried."

He was relieved to be talking about a topic as mundane as animals. All this settling down nonsense made him feel restless. As though he needed to get back to base and chase down those deployment orders for their next mission. If only a single signature didn't stand in his way.

"So Blitzen adopted him?" Mason offered.

A warm smile spread across Holly's face, and he found he quite enjoyed how it illuminated her eyes. "Something like that."

Through a clearing of old evergreens, the faded red boards of the barn appeared. Snow coated the roof as well as the split rail fence that ran along the perimeter. Mason recalled a couple of seasons baling hay and unloading it in this very barn. It could hold quite the number of large bales.

Though he wanted to know more, they found themselves right outside the barn. He was here to work, he reminded himself. Good ol' manual labor on the ranch he'd considered a second home ought to help his situation. It *had* to. "This is bigger than I remember." It seemed smaller during his teenage years.

"I'm thinking it can hold about a hundred people." Holly slipped through the door, only holding it for a second for him to follow before he could ask what she meant by that comment. Surely they weren't cleaning this out so they could house *people* in it?

"I guess—" But whatever thought Mason had slipped away as a memory carried its way back to him. The rope that dangled from a far center rafter took him back more than a decade. He was transported to the time Paul conned him into sneaking in to swing on the rope into hay bales. Mr. Maxwell hadn't been too pleased the next morning to discover the disrupted hay. The boys admitted their guilt, since their arms were covered in scratches.

" . . . list I've made. It's long, but there's nothing on here too terrible." She chuckled, making him realize he'd missed some of her joke.

"The list." He steadied his breathing that'd become erratic, forcing himself back to the present. Fighting to keep his expression blank. Unreadable. He wasn't prepared for the punch packed at the memories of his best friend. Paul West helped make his life bearable after his parents were killed. He missed him more now that he was back in Starlight and felt his absence everywhere.

Paul had been killed in action. Losing his best friend had driven Mason to join the Special Forces. He wanted to do more. Save more lives.

Holly removed her gloves, shoved a hand into her oversized coat pocket, and pulled out a folded paper. She handed it to him and gave him a moment to browse the several items, reminding him of the task at hand. "How long do you think it'll take to get through everything? I'll help, of course. And Bobby offered to give us an hour here and there if we need it. But we'll be shorthanded next week, so we've only got him through Friday. He's not free this weekend, either."

"Bobby?" A cousin, if he recalled the right boy. Well, man now. "Collins?"

"That's the one." Holly's eyes fell back on the paper he still held, eager to get to work, no doubt.

Mason scanned it again, then the barn to identify the different tasks and what they might entail. "Couple of days."

"Days?" Holly repeated, her eyes wide. "As in two days, not weeks?"

He shrugged, uncertain where her concern originated. He'd do most of the work. It'd be good. Therapeutic. Hopefully help strengthen the weakened muscles in his leg. The only unfortunate piece to this realization was that he would find himself restless and bored very soon.

"You want me to take longer?"

She shook her head. "No, no, definitely not. This is just . . . it's better news than I expected."

"What are you going to do with this barn anyway?" He'd tried to ask at least three times, but every time had found interruption. He waited for the dog to bark or her cell to ring. But nothing came except the rush of red to Holly's cheeks.

"I may have promised to host a dance here. Well, to rent it out as a venue for a dance."

Mason scanned the dusty barn, covered in a layer of loose hay, cobwebs, and dust. “When?”

“Christmas Eve.”

If he’d been drinking coffee, he would’ve choked on it for sure. “That’s pretty soon.” Cleaning out the barn? That could be accomplished with ease. But the rest was a tall order. Snow piled in one corner where the roof needed a patch. Half the floor was dirt. Could they manage to get all the dust out?

“It’s a huge project, I know.” Holly sat back onto a rickety table Mason wouldn’t have trusted with a coffee mug. The defeated look in her eyes tore at him. Maybe it was a renewed sense of purpose, but he found himself desperate to make that look disappear.

“Let me get started, then.” He looked toward the tractor. He could move it and the hay bales together. Sweeping would have to be done multiple times, but it was a mindless chore. “Once it’s cleaned out, we need to talk repairs. Upgrades.” Their eyes met over the cloud his voice made in the chilly barn. “Heat.” There was certainly a lot to do, but it gave Mason a sense of relief that he’d stay busy.

“You know I can’t pay you?” Holly reminded him.

“I know.”

He looked her up and down, impressed that she came dressed to work. Jeans, cowgirl boots that appeared quite worn, a flannel-lined denim jacket and work gloves. "Let's get to it, then."

The sun had gone down over two hours ago. All of Mason's muscles ached. Even his fingers struggled to grip the thick slice of pizza in his hand. But with the fresh ingredients and thick flaky crust, he'd suffer through the pain. "This is tasty," he told Holly. He could appreciate a good pizza when he met one.

She'd showered. In her blue snowman pajama pants and hoodie, she looked quite comfortable. Her ebony hair, wavy, hung a few inches past her shoulders, the shoulders of her sweatshirt damp with moisture. He'd have said she looked relaxed if the worry lines etched across her forehead weren't so prominent. It made him wonder about the crumpled wads of paper in the office.

"Sorry there's not more than carryout to eat. I've been meaning to get to the store."

He thought back to the nearly empty pantry he discovered that morning and wondered if she disliked cooking or simply didn't have the time. Seemed he wondered a lot of things about Holly Maxwell. *Too many, perhaps.* "No complaints here. This is really good."

"Best pizza in Starlight."

"Pizza this good makes a man think about moving back, you know." It was meant as a joke, because he could never think about moving back to Starlight on any serious level. Or settling anywhere for that matter. But something flashed in Holly's brown eyes and it made him pause. "Except, I have an obligation."

"Army commitment and all that." Holly offered a smile, but it didn't reach her eyes. She quickly looked away and studied the notepad in front of her.

He wiped his fingers with a napkin and wadded it up. "Yeah." Though if the doc wouldn't clear him to go back to duty, he wasn't sure what his future held.

She scratched some items from her list, added others. Tapping her pencil against the kitchen island, she said, "I hope you're prepared for the work ahead. It's quite the project."

"I couldn't handle sitting around idle all day," he admitted. "Any chance you have an extra vehicle I could borrow? Need to make a trip into town soon." He hated to ask. If he had his way, he would've driven a rental from the airport, but Brantley had been pretty insistent that family didn't need to do that. His grandma taught him never to be too proud to accept hospitality when it was offered from a place of kindness and love.

He wished she were still here. Even now, more

than five years later, he still yearned for their long phone conversations. The holidays in Starlight wouldn't be the same without her.

"I'd loan you my truck, but I'll be doing a lot of running around this week." She bit on the corner of her lip until she lifted her gaze. "There *is* an old truck no one's using. Isn't the most reliable, though."

Mason wasn't one to be picky. He didn't much care for the feeling of being trapped on a ranch. At the very least, he wanted to pick up some groceries so the two of them wouldn't starve. Mario's Pizza was pretty amazing, but neither of them needed to rely on it solely. "Does it run?"

"Last I checked. Starter acts up sometimes. And the heater doesn't always kick on. But it's four-wheel drive."

"I know my way around a wrench a little. I think I can manage."

Holly reached for a napkin and dabbed at the corners of her lips. He had to force himself to look away. "What is it you *do* in the army exactly?" she asked.

"Crew chief." It wasn't a lie. He'd been just that before he joined the Special Forces. But it didn't seem like a detail relevant to their current conversation. If he couldn't get a handle on his leg and his insomnia, he wouldn't be going back to the Green Berets anyway.

She reached for another slice. "What does that mean?"

Blitzen sat at the window, watching Norbert as the cow chomped away at the dinner Holly had prepared him. He wondered if Norbert appreciated the luxuries he'd been given, the pal always concerned about him. The pair amused and confused him. "It's a fancy way of saying you're a Blackhawk pilot's rearview mirror."

"I've never ridden in a helicopter before. Sounds fun."

Mason was impressed that she knew what a Blackhawk was. Seemed a lot of folks didn't. "It has its perks."

It wasn't until Holly carried the empty pizza box to the trash that he realized how ravenous he'd been. She hadn't touched more than two slices. "North Carolina the only place you've been?" she asked.

"Was in Alaska before that. With Paul and Brantley."

"Ah, that's right."

"Got lucky enough to stay there for six years," he offered before she could ask. The three had been stationed there together prior to the deployment that claimed Paul's life. "I have to admit, it's kind of neat to see a moose from the inside of a helicopter."

"A moose?"

Maybe his tactic was a cheap trick, but he wasn't ready to talk about anything too serious. Not tonight.

The last thing he wanted was for anyone to know about his dilemma and pity him. "I'll have to find a picture. I have one on my phone somewhere." He pushed back from his chair, suddenly feeling restless.

"I'd like to see that." She returned to her notepad and carried it, along with that same paperback from last night, toward the office. "Maybe tomorrow?"

He nodded, relieved she didn't expect his company all evening. A normal man would shower and get some rest. Though they'd accomplished a lot on the barn today, there was still plenty to do. "Meet you at the barn in the morning?" he asked.

"How does seven sound?"

Too late. "Perfect."

"See you then?"

He nodded. "I might check out that truck if you don't mind?"

"Go for it. It's parked outside the main garage. Keys inside. No promises." She gave him a wink that left him with a confused smile as Blitzen trailed down the hall after her. Claws click-clacked on the laminate flooring. Surely, the wink didn't mean anything.

Once layered up to ward off as much of the night chill as he could, Mason trudged through the snow, deeper on the side of the garage where it had drifted. He found the old red Ford buried in drifts up to the tops of the tires.

His dad had owned an old F-250 like this. As a

boy, he spent hours on the driveway lying on his back watching his old man with a socket wrench. He wondered if this truck leaked as much oil as that one had.

"I thought you might need this." Holly's voice startled him, but he caught himself before he went over backwards into a snowdrift. She held out a shovel, but he hardly saw it through the woman in a stocking hat and pajama pants tucked into fluffy boots. She made quite the adorable sight, and he wasn't prepared for his temporary loss of breath.

"Thanks." To ward off the ridiculous reaction, he immediately went to work shoveling. Holly Maxwell was off limits; that's all there was to that.

After half a dozen scoops, he realized she hadn't left. Norbert and Blitzen both stood at her side now, heads mutually tilted in curiosity at the stranger with a shovel.

"You need anything? Coffee? Hot cider?"

"Nope." He went back to digging, eager to be rid of her now that she seemed so reluctant to say what was really on her mind. The longer she lingered, the more likely she was to spit it out, and he wasn't sure he was ready for whatever it was. "Thanks, though."

"Mason, I—"

"You're shivering."

Holly looked down at her arms folded across her chest, as if to confirm he was telling the truth. "It's cold out," she admitted.

"You should go inside before you catch cold." He sounded a lot like his grandmother, and it made him smile. But that faded quickly as realization dawned that Grandma too was no longer here to visit. Everything about the only town that ever felt like home now felt different. Foreign.

Perhaps returning to Starlight was the worst thing he could've done.

But deep down inside, he knew that was a lie. Mason hoped the cure to his problems lay hidden in Starlight.

"I'm not as helpless as you think."

That stopped his shoveling efforts again. "Holly Maxwell, of all the words out there to describe you, helpless is the last I'd choose." He recalled more than one rainy, miserable day moving cattle. She'd stuck it out right beside them on her own horse without a single complaint. Which was more than could be said for a couple of her male cousins.

"Good. I'm glad we got that straightened out."

He waited again for her to retreat inside, but she and the furry duo stood side by side. "There's a spot in the garage if you need it. Tools, too."

"Is there?" Feelings warred inside him about whether he wanted her to go or stay. *Go.* He should want her to go. *Stay.*

"I'll open the garage door."

Norbert trailed after her, more like a dog than he'd ever witnessed a cow behave. Blitzen raced a circle around the garage before reappearing at the door. It wasn't until the garage door hummed that he realized he'd been staring after her. Try as he may to shake away the thought, he was afraid he just might be in trouble where Holly Maxwell was concerned.

CHAPTER 7

Holly

Holly was used to a quiet kitchen in the morning, aside from Blitzen lying on the rug watching her bounce around. Sooner or later, he knew she'd break and toss one of his favorite treats his way. She was grateful for her continued solitude, despite Mason in the house. Seemed he was antisocial in the mornings, and that was okay with her.

She and Mason had managed to back the truck into a garage space, but one of the starter bolts nearly came off in the process. They were up past eleven working on it. Well, Holly mostly handed him tools as he worked beneath it.

Mason.

The odd turn of events had again kept her up half the night. Potent enough to make reading anything beyond her first chapter assignment impossible. Before she could successfully take a bite of her peanut butter and jelly sandwich, a yawn escaped, loud enough to startle Blitzen from his lazy position on the rug.

"So much for getting ahead," she muttered. Chapter one hadn't been helpful at all when it came to the Christmas gala barn dreamed up by their local author. Holly'd been prepared to make a list, but the notebook remained blank. The dance was but a whispered thought in the main character's head this early in the story.

"Sorry, Blitz. First I have to see about a wolf." She eyed her half-eaten sandwich, musing over the text Brantley had sent her earlier. A wolf, just what they needed. "Then, if there's time, I think this morning might call for freshly baked muffins."

It was early enough that Holly didn't want to wake Mason. He was probably used to predawn mornings in the army, but he was on leave, and they'd been up much too late. Seemed only fair to let the man sleep before she put him to work today.

She slipped out the front door to meet Brantley, who was waiting in the driveway with an ATV running. One of the best investments they made this year was the two enclosed ATVs with heaters. At least, Holly considered them wise investments before the storm wiped out most of the wheat crop. Now she hoped she wouldn't have to sell them.

"Brought you fresh coffee," Brantley said with a yawn. "Courtesy of Jillian."

"Thanks." She closed the door and let the warm, caramel-flavored liquid tingle her tongue and warm her entire body. She'd hardly set the cup down before he sped off down the frozen, bumpy drive. Thank goodness for lids.

The north pasture was a ten-minute drive from the house in ideal weather conditions. Today, it might take twenty. A fresh layer of frost and ice coated the road and ditches. "Who spotted the wolf?" she asked. There'd been no report of lost cattle.

"Jeremy. Caught her feasting on a rabbit yesterday. He kept watch last night."

"Good." They couldn't afford to let that hungry wolf near the livestock, even in the best of conditions. With the state of things now . . . "She's probably got cubs to feed?"

"That's what we're thinking." As they bounced along, the two discussed the situation, possible solutions, and how they planned to keep the cows safe and hopefully remove the wolf threat altogether. It was the first time Holly felt like a good manager in weeks. If they succeeded at this, maybe it'd be the start to turning around.

"How's it been with Mason in the house?"

Brantley asked as they slowed to take a trail along the fence, catching her off guard with the sudden change of subject.

"Good." With the sun still asleep beneath the horizon, at least the blush on her cheeks was hidden. It was ridiculous how easily her schoolgirl crush emerged with hardly more than a mere mention of Mason's name. "He's a pretty quiet houseguest."

"Hear you've got him roped into a project."

"He wanted something to do."

"You're really going to rent that barn out for some Christmas dance?"

She couldn't blame the skepticism that hung in Brantley's tone. If Trish or Lina were to stop by today to confirm their reservation, they'd surely cancel and laugh all the way back to the Holbrook Ranch. "That's the plan."

"Good luck."

Box of muffins from Millie's Bakery in one hand and drink carrier with two large coffees in the other, Holly pushed the side door to the barn open with a solid shove of her hip. They hadn't found the wolf, but they did have a plan to keep watch. She felt better for it.

Before she was across the threshold, both Norbert and Blitzen came blazing by, tails wagging.

At least, it looked an awful lot like Norbert's tail was wagging.

"Good morning," she greeted, happy to see that Mason was already in the barn and ready to get to work. "I brought—" It took only moments for her eyes to catch all the improvements. The clean floors, lack of garden tools, missing hay bales, absent cobwebs. "Mason, did you do all of this?"

"I got an early start."

"You even moved the tractor. I didn't think it would run." Holly chided herself for not checking the barn after scouting for the wolf. A short detour would've alerted her to the lights. She felt guilty now for not coming straight to the barn after her chores with Brantley were wrapped up, though peanut butter and jelly for breakfast wouldn't have satisfied either of them. "You didn't have to do all this!" She spun in a full circle, completely in shock. Surely this was a dream. It had to be.

"Finished your list." He handed the piece of notebook paper back to her. "Started a new one for the repairs we need to do. Hope you don't mind."

No way one man could clean out the *entire* thing in one morning. "You made your own list?" Holly's smile stretched her cheeks a little too much, but she didn't care. "A man after my own heart." She spun away from him as quickly as the words slipped out, lest he read too much into what she said.

Holly scanned the new list.

Corner roof repair.

Replace rotted ceiling sections.

Fix loose electrical sockets.

Replace broken glass pane.

Reinforce table legs.

"I assume you want to finish the floor too?" Mason asked, pulling her attention from the other half dozen items he jotted down. The dollars had already begun to add up in her head, and she didn't like what it might cost to pull this off. It was sure to exceed the thousand dollars Trish promised as a rental fee.

"There's old barn wood for that in the spare shed." She hoped it hadn't all rotted. "It'll match what's already down, I think." She'd considered giving their local home renovation expert a call to confirm her idea would work—because she certainly couldn't afford to hire *the* Ronnie Ross—but she'd gotten the idea from watching one of the local reality TV star's shows.

Mason's drawn eyebrows suggested he wasn't convinced. "I'll take a look after lunch." Lines crinkled at the corners of his tired eyes, and she found herself unable to look away.

"You couldn't have gotten much sleep." Three, maybe four hours. Tops.

"Jetlag."

But she didn't believe him. "Mason, I'm impressed with how much you accomplished. In shock, really. I'm not even sure how you're standing upright. I thought this would take us all week. Maybe you should take a nap."

"I'm fine." He shifted his weight from his right leg to his left. Holly swore she caught a flashing wince of pain, but he erased the expression so quickly she couldn't be sure. "What's next?"

She scanned his list again, unable to meet those intense eyes. Mason's gaze had always intimidated her. Made her feel exposed. Seemed it still had the ability to make her blush like a teenager. "Looks like we need to round up supplies." She let out a defeated sigh she was unsuccessful at hiding. There wasn't enough money for all of this. The rental fee was only one grand *if* Trish signed off on the barn as her venue. The items on this list were surely double that, if not more.

"What is it?" Mason's voice, deep but compassionate, soothed her anxiety-ridden pulse, if only momentarily. She longed to confess the true extent of the ranch's financial problems to *someone*. She almost told him all of it.

Almost. "I already went to town once this morning. Guess we'll need to make another trip."

"I bet you have more on the ranch than you realize. No need to spend money on things you already have, right?"

The air felt a little lighter at that realization. She could breathe again, at least for the moment. "Right."

"Show me around." He waved toward the door, catching the attention of Blitzen. Norbert trailed after him, too. The red ball bounced along with them right through the open door.

Holly laughed at Mason's drawn eyebrows. "It's just easier to let them go first."

"You need to record this or something."

She stepped outside as Mason held the door open for her, a gesture that hadn't been bestowed upon her in ages. Seemed she'd become too much *one of the crew* for any of that business. And the last disaster-date she'd been on, *she* held the door.

Holly quickly shook away thoughts of dating. "So I've been told."

As she trudged through the packed down snow to the toolshed, Mason reached for her elbow and pulled her back. Unprepared for the change in direction or the contact, she tripped over her own two feet. Arms flailed as she attempted to right herself and Mason tried—unsuccessfully—to catch her.

Holly knocked them both into a snowbank. When they landed, her face lay cradled in the crook of his arm, a protective arm wrapped securely around her shoulders. She stiffened with embarrassment until the vibration of his laughter shook her snow-free cheek.

Blitzen rushed over, licking her in the face to make sure she was okay. "Thanks for the concern, Blitz. We're alive."

Mason laughed all the way to his feet, pulling her up with him. Embarrassment dissipated as her own laughter took over. "I wanted to show you I brought the truck. Didn't expect to get tackled over it."

"The truck." Shoulders shaking, he nodded toward the old Ford that blended in with the barn. Within minutes, they'd laughed so much her belly ached and she was forced to wipe away a tear.

"You were so eager to walk everywhere." Something close to a twinkle danced in Mason's eyes, leaving Holly tongue-tied. He was usually the serious one; even as a teenager, he never seemed to have time for things like small talk or teasing. Always prepared to get to work. To get things done. She quite liked this side of him.

"I suppose it *is* a little much to assume we'd carry everything back."

The playful look they shared caused her pulse to shoot up like a rocket launching. She hurried toward the truck, eager to hide her face. This was a problem. This was a *big* problem. How could they be flirting? Surely, she was reading too much into this.

Norbert zipped by in pursuit of the red ball. "I don't know how I'm going to explain him to Grandpa," she told Mason, because he'd caught up to her with ease. The man had purposeful strides that made quick time of any distance. Though he'd always been that way, the army had obviously turned that up a notch.

"Have you tried moving him back with the other calves?"

"Once." Holly hated to remember that night. Blitzen had whined at the back-porch door until dawn. If losing a night of sleep wasn't bad enough, she discovered the bottom half of that door scratched halfway through. "Let's just say it didn't go well."

"Maybe Norbert will grow on your grandpa." Mason nudged her with his shoulder, and she looked up to find him actually smiling. "He grew on me."

Holly wanted to feel a shred of hope, but Grandpa was all business. Cattle were raised to produce an income. "I've never named a cow before," she admitted as they reached the truck. "Grandpa always warned me not to get attached."

She climbed in and waited for him to do the same, crossing her fingers beneath the sleeve of her heavy jacket that it started.

"You won't be able to sell him, you know."

Norbert wasn't even a year old. Holly had purposefully put off any thought of what his future might hold. "Blitzen would be crushed." But how could she justify keeping any of the herd after how this last season went? *At some point* . . . She shoved away those thoughts. How could one *not* get attached to Norbert?

"Hey." Mason reached across the truck, placing

his hand on hers. Without their gloves, the heat of his touch had no barrier. She sucked in a breath, certain she'd spontaneously combust. "You'll figure something out. You always do, Holl."

His rough fingers slid from the top of her hand as he started the truck. The first and second cranks weren't successful. "Does Norbert know to get out of the way?"

"Yeah. Blitzen's taught him almost everything he knows." Again, she yearned to tell Mason about the state of the ranch. The real *why* behind going to the lengths she did to save Norbert. But before she could decide, the old truck roared to life, making conversation impossible.

No one, Mason included, deserved to carry that burden with her. She created the mess; she'd find the way out.

CHAPTER 8

Mason

The days passed in a blur of chilly weather and hard work. Mason had no more than blinked and he'd been at the Maxwell Ranch for a week. Despite his continuous inability to sleep more than an hour or two at a time, he kept busy enough to pass the time. Maybe one day soon it would all catch up with him and knock him out cold for three days straight.

He could hope.

Until then, he'd continue helping Holly with whatever she had to keep him moving.

He had to give her props. She spent every day out in the barn with him, on top of seeing to her other responsibilities around the ranch. He wondered how much sleep she purposely sacrificed during those late nights in her office. She was definitely her grandpa's granddaughter.

Though he'd been avoiding the office or any room that might alert Holly to his sleeplessness during the middle of the night, tonight he desperately needed a different book. The one he took in haste his first night was about nineteenth-century sailing. If that couldn't put him to sleep, nothing would.

"You're still up?" he asked, fighting to hide a limp. His leg ached more than usual today, no doubt from finally slowing down.

Holly sat hunched over a ledger, thumb rubbing her temple. She let out a sigh before she looked up. The lines around her eyes shone more prominently under the glow of the overhead light. "Things to do, you know." The accumulation of crumpled paper on her desk and in the overflowing trash can seemed to suggest the list was quite long. "Good book?"

Lifting the hardbound book at her, he said, "Not really my taste."

She pushed back her chair and stood in a stretch accompanied by a yawn loud enough to startle a sleeping Blitzen from his dog bed in the corner. He lazily lifted his head, scanned the room, wagged his tail twice at the sight of Mason, and then dozed right back to sleep.

"Didn't take you for the sailing type." Holly took

the book from him and placed it back on the shelf. Instead of her favorite snowman pajamas, she still donned jeans and a pair of mismatched Christmas socks, one red with Christmas trees, one green with reindeer.

"You seem a little tired."

Her cute smirk faded into a weak smile. "That barn . . . it's been a chore."

He wasn't fooled. There was something unsaid in those words. Something that very possibly lay hidden in the crumpled papers that filled the metal trash can beside the desk. They tempted him to sneak back down in a couple of hours to see what secrets they held.

"Got you wearing two different socks?" he teased. Then he instantly chided himself. He had to stop flirting. This could go nowhere with Holly.

"The matches both disappeared."

"Maybe you should get some rest?"

"Did you want another book?"

He did, but it seemed pointless. He wouldn't be able to concentrate on words tonight. All this manual labor had yet to knock him out for one single night of solid sleep. Every night that passed made him more anxious that he'd never be able to return to duty. Would the army even keep him as an instructor or platoon sergeant in an aviation unit if he couldn't get a handle on this?

"I'll pass tonight. Tired, you know." He lingered,

though he couldn't understand why. They'd worked well together all week, but they were no more than family friends. "When does Amelia get in?"

"Should be any day now." Holly dropped into her chair and opened her ledger to the spot where she left off. It was no surprise that Lawrence Maxwell hadn't upgraded to tracking such things on a computer. He'd always been reluctant to trust technology, and it seemed he'd passed the trait along to his granddaughter. "I'll ask Brantley in the morning. I have to ride out with him to check on the wolf situation again."

"Wolf?"

"Yeah. Just what we need, huh?" She gave that weak smile again, and he very much wanted to ask what the truth of it all was. Because there was quite a lot Holly wasn't telling him. But Mason couldn't ask that of her with his own secrets buried so deep.

"You staying up much longer?"

"I just have to write down a few numbers. Go over a few things."

"It'll all be there in the morning." He wasn't one to talk, but she looked so tired. So run ragged.

"Afraid I'll mix up the numbers?" she teased. But there was something serious hidden in that tone.

"Is everything okay, Holl?" He wasn't sure when he'd started calling her *Holl* instead of Holly. But anymore, he couldn't seem to help himself. Her cheeks flashed pink each time he did, and he found he quite enjoyed that. It didn't mean anything beyond that. It couldn't.

"Yeah, of course. Just a lot to do before Grandpa and Grandma Charlotte get back. Plus, this barn thing . . ." She waved toward a paperback he'd seen a few times. The one the local author wrote.

"Anything I can do to help?"

Her immediate instinct was to decline. He could tell by the way her lips instantly parted to tell him just that. But her gaze locked on the book, and slowly those lips fell closed. Those chocolatey eyes sparkled with renewed energy. "Actually, there is something."

"Name it."

"I know you said you're not looking for a new book right now . . ."

"But?"

He'd tried at least three times to read that book about sailing, but the prose was old and dry and the topic was even dryer. He'd never sailed on a boat. Never wanted to. The instructional novel had quite turned him off of reading for the foreseeable future.

"How do you feel about Christmas?"

Mason was caught off guard by the question. Christmas was something he hadn't given much attention to in years. A little when his grandma was still alive, but otherwise, Christmas all those years ago on the Maxwell Ranch was a faint memory tucked away. "I'm not Scrooge, if that's what you're asking." But truthfully, he kind of was.

"This dance. It's a Christmas Eve gala based on the one in *this* book."

He looked back and forth between Holly and the book she held up at him. "You want me to read this?" Confusion swam through his mind. He'd been more than happy to clear out the old barn, clean it up, repair what was broken, install the new flooring. But decorating it? He shook his head. "I'm not really the interior décor type."

With a deep breath, she confessed, "I've only read two chapters."

"Two good chapters, I hope."

Holly shook her head, exhaustion swimming through those beautiful eyes of hers. He yearned to do something—anything—to take that burden from her. He was helpless not to want that. "I—"

If he wasn't mistaken, tears welled in the corners of her eyes. In a beat, he was at her side, sitting on the desk, facing her. He reached for her hands and held them securely in his own. Doing it all without a premeditated thought. "Holl, talk to me."

Her fingers trembled in his own, and he waited for the tears that couldn't be held back. They trailed down her cheeks moments later. "The ranch . . ." She took a deep breath, closed her eyes, finally pulling her fingers free from his. He immediately felt the absence of her touch.

"Yeah?"

She refused to meet his eyes, staring straight ahead into nothing. "It's bad, Mason."

"What's bad?"

Blitzen chose that moment to scramble to his feet, barking thunderously as he charged to the front door.

Nothing short of sheer panic flashed through Holly's eyes. "Someone's here." She shoved out of her chair, swiping at her eyes with fervor. "It's after midnight. Who's here?" She spun in a circle, searching for something.

Mason could only guess it was a mirror. He reached for her wrist and pulled her gently to face him. "Here, let me." His thumbs brushed away the moisture under her eyes, along with a light film of mascara. Wet eyelashes blinked onto the tips of his fingers as she looked up at him.

For the first time, he didn't force himself to look away from her lips. He'd been in denial if he told himself he didn't think of kissing Holly. They'd spent so much time together this past week. Worked hard, side by side. He admired her resilient work ethic and refusal to complain about anything.

"The door . . ." Holly pulled free. In the doorway, she stopped and turned to him. "Can we just forget this happened? No one needs to know I was crying into the ledgers."

Though disappointment hit him harder than expected, he nodded. "Of course."

He let her go answer the door, equally curious who might be arriving in the middle of the night. Maybe Aunt Amelia was able to fly out a couple of days early. Or Lawrence and Charlotte returned from their trip ahead of schedule.

Mason lingered in the kitchen for only a few seconds. Though Holly was likely not in any danger, his protective instinct wouldn't allow her to face the unknown alone. Not this late at night. With Blitzen at his ankles, he weaved his way toward the front of the house.

By the time he made it to the entry hall, she'd opened the door. A tall, thin man in a grease-stained baseball cap stood on the porch, draped in a Carhartt jacket. "I put her up with Jillian and Brantley tonight," he heard the man say. It wasn't until the man lifted his eyes toward Mason that recognition hit.

"Bobby?"

"Mason Montgomery. I heard you were hanging around for the holidays." Bobby stepped across the threshold, and Holly closed the door behind him. A cold spot lingered in the entryway, enough to see a couple of her breaths.

He and Bobby shook hands, but any small talk was cut short.

"You're sure it's shot?" Holly's expression remained blank, but Mason didn't miss the worry lines in her otherwise smooth forehead. Blitzen plopped down at her feet, leaning against her legs. Seemed the dog could sense the troubled worries of his owner. She absently traced the top of his head with her fingers.

"I've been tinkering with it for the last two hours, tried everything I could think of. It's not spitting out a lick of heat. If you want to call someone—"

"No. If you can't fix it, then it's done for." Holly let out a breath, a calculated look in her eyes. "Any idea about replacement cost?"

"It was an old unit. We'll probably need to upgrade to something newer."

Mason's trained military eye caught Holly's shoulders stiffen. The urge to take her hand swept over him, and he had to force it away. This was her ranch, and he wasn't about to step on her toes in front of anyone. Even if Bobby was family, he was still employed by Holly. "Can you get me an estimate tomorrow?"

"Sure thing. Sorry to come over with bad news. Thought I'd wake you, but—"

"Anything I can do to help?" Mason interjected. He doubted any of Holly's crew knew how many hours she spent at the desk after all the chores were finished.

"Already got a couple of space heaters going on the pipes," Bobby answered.

"So, not much we can do until morning." A yawn

escaped Holly, her eyes watering. "Our guest?" she asked Bobby.

"Jillian set her up in their guest room tonight. Tomorrow she's planning to spend the morning at that coffee shop. Said she'd check on things after lunch."

"Good. Thank you, Bobby."

Her cousin nodded, heading for the door. "Oh, one more thing. The red ATV needs a new starter."

"Thanks, Bobby."

Norbert rushed to the window, watching Bobby until his taillights faded down the winding drive.

Mason should leave well enough alone. Holly had proven more than once in the last week that she had everything under control. But he couldn't shake the feeling that something more was beneath the surface. "What was all that about, if you don't mind me asking?"

She let out a groan, fists balling at her sides. Three deep breaths later, she finally answered him with a calm, collected tone. "We have a couple of guests staying in our extra cabins."

"Like the one I was going to—"

"Yeah." Holly locked the deadbolt. "These are paying guests. Writers on deadlines. Don't exactly want to inconvenience them."

"There's not much you can do about the heat going out." Mason was forced to follow her into the kitchen. He watched from the doorway as she searched the sparse cupboards, retrieving a mostly empty peanut butter jar and two heels—the last remnants of a loaf of bread. "Seems Bobby has it covered."

"They paid good money for peace and quiet." She slathered peanut butter on one side. "And *heat*."

Mason fished a jar of jelly out of the fridge. Tomorrow, he'd get a few meals' worth of groceries. This peanut butter and jelly obsession had to end. Holly worked much too hard to come home to a simple sandwich or takeout at the end of the day. "Did you want me to read that book, then?"

The first hint of relief flashed through her eyes. "Would you? I think the book club will do most of the decorating, but we should be prepared to help. Can't imagine any of them will want to hang lights from the rafters."

Though reading a Christmas romance of all things didn't exactly appeal to his masculine nature, he'd treat it like research. He longed to reassure her that whatever was troubling her most would be okay. Instead, he folded his arms across his chest and offered a smirk. "Someone has to do it."

CHAPTER 9

Holly

"I can't wait to see it!" Lina Holbrook gushed outside the barn. Her bright smile could've illuminated the entire state of Wyoming on a dark night.

Though Holly forced a smile, dread filled her. *What if she doesn't like it?* What if Lina walked through that door and her face dropped? Though Trish obviously had the final say on the venue, Lina was definitely a gatekeeper. Holly and Mason—mostly Mason—had spent almost all of their daylight hours, and some of their nighttime hours—bringing the barn back to life.

But no matter what they did, it was still just a barn.

"I don't have anything inside. No decorations or anything, so you'll have to use your imagination."

"Oh, that's no bother at all!" Lina practically bolted inside the second Mason held the door open.

Christmas Eve was hardly a week away. If Trish liked the barn, would that be enough time for them to spread word about the event? Turning the barn into a venue this one time was only the beginning. Her grandpa would never approve unless she had a solid plan to turn it into a regular revenue stream.

"Relax." Mason reached for her hand as she walked by and gave it a squeeze, stealing the very breath from her lungs.

How many times as a hopelessly romantic girl had she daydreamed this very scenario? Holly tried to push away any silly feelings she might have, but she couldn't deny the comfort she felt with her hand in his. Or how much she didn't want to let go.

"There's still so much to do," Holly said, trying to sound confident through the anxiety. Even though the hard part seemed over, she'd never let the book club women do everything on their own. She'd find time to help put up trees and lights. Track down decorations they might have a hard time finding.

Mason winked at her. "Lucky for you, someone read the book."

The first sense of relief she'd had in weeks washed over her. She had every intention of reading the book, really she had. But time was her enemy lately. She'd been avoiding Jillian this week and her demands for chapter-by-chapter reports. "That was fast."

"I don't really have another speed setting."

She chuckled at that, finding she enjoyed his humor. She'd miss it when he returned to duty. "Thank you, Mason."

"Better get inside before Lina gets too carried away."

"Yeah."

Reluctantly, she dropped his hand. Tingles danced along her fingers from his touch.

"I'm right behind you," he said.

"This is magnificent!" Lina exclaimed, turning wide, excited eyes to Holly. "Trish will absolutely love this. All the ladies will. This space is perfect."

"I think it could hold up to a hundred people." Holly had no idea how big the gala in the book was, but surely that detail wasn't the most important. The barn wasn't an exact replica, and the crowd they held would ultimately be determined by the fire marshal.

Lina moved about the room, using her hands to paint invisible pictures as she went. "This is where the biggest tree should go." She stopped and peered directly overhead. "With mistletoe dangling from the rafter, of course. That's where Jenny and Pete shared their kiss, remember?"

"Yes, of course," Holly said. Because she had to say *something*.

"I'll grab the ladder after we're done so it's ready to use when we need it," Mason jumped in. "We'll need to get some lights up on those rafters, too. Might as well do that while we're hanging mistletoe."

Holly sent him a grateful smile, mouthing *thank you* just out of sight of Lina. "You think we can sell enough tickets to make this worthwhile?" She hated to be the realist who dimmed any elation, but she had to know. The success of this event would determine the future of this barn.

"Oh, I have no doubt. There's already quite the buzz in town, including Trish's fan base."

"Will she be stopping by to check out the barn?"

"She's on a deadline for her next book. Something about a stubborn male character who refuses to talk to her." Lina rolled her eyes. "But she promised to steal a few minutes today and meet me out here. I have absolutely no doubt she will be in love with this space. It's so perfect."

Holly didn't know much about writing books or their characters, but she was quite familiar with *ideas* not speaking to her. The mountain of crumpled paper in her office defended that argument.

A knock on the side door drew everyone's attention. "Ah, that'll be her now," Lina said.

Trish approached the group in slow steps as she took in the barn. Her smile grew with each step. "Did you tell them?" She looked at her grandma expectantly.

The question instantly put Holly on edge. She wasn't sure she could take any more surprises. Not today. Maybe not until next year.

Lina patted Trish on the shoulder. "I thought I'd leave that to you. Wanted to make sure you approved of the barn first." Her expression gave nothing away and Holly braced for whatever curveball was headed her way. Did they need to somehow build a stage? Change the light fixtures? Repaint the exterior?

"Oh, absolutely I do! This is perfect." Trish clapped her hands together.

"Isn't it, though?" Lina agreed.

"What was it you needed to tell me?" Holly asked, because the suspense nibbled at her. She wanted to get the mysterious obstacle out in the open *now* so she could make a plan to overcome it.

"I'm on a teeny tiny deadline for this next book," Trish said, offering a pleading smile. "See, one of my characters won't talk to me. He's a real standoffish sort of guy, and he decided to extend his charming personality trait to the author."

Holly wasn't sure where this was going, but suspected the workload on her plate was about to get heavier.

Unzipping her purse, Trish pulled out a check and handed it to Holly. "This is the deposit on the venue, as promised. We absolutely love the space."

"Sounds like there's a *but*," Mason said, reminding everyone, including Holly, that he was still there. She felt comforted by his presence. He'd still be there after the news was delivered and the women left. She let herself breathe easy at that thought.

"Not really a but . . . More like an addition."

"Oh?" Holly asked.

"You've read the book, right?"

Oh, crap. *Back on the spot.* She wouldn't admit she hadn't read the book. That would be the quickest way to lose her first and only barn venue client. And throw away all the money they'd already invested in fixing it up. Grandpa would *not* be impressed.

"It's a fun story," Mason said, turning all heads his way. "Holly insisted I read it, since it's by a Starlight author. Not usually my type of book, but it's good. Very Christmas-y. You sure love mistletoe."

"I do," Trish admitted.

Saved again by Mason. Holly wished she could pay him for all the work he'd done the past week. Wished she could do something to thank him.

"Could you recreate it?" Trish's eyes were wide and hopeful. Maybe even a little desperate. "I won't possibly have time to do that and get this book finished on schedule. This deadline . . ."

"I—" Holly couldn't find words. They'd spent a solid week getting that barn cleaned out and fixed up. She'd neglected a lot of her other duties to do that. She had a list for lists she needed just to get caught up again.

"I'm willing to offer a sizable bonus."

"We have a lot of the decorations already rounded up," Lina offered. "You'll need to track down a few more Christmas trees, nutcrackers, and some ornaments. But we rounded up enough strings of lights to illuminate the entire town. Also, Peggy's Petal Paradise has all the mistletoe you'll need. Just needs to be picked up."

Holly scrambled to jot everything down, missing words and entire list items, she was sure. She pushed away the dread that tried to take over. She could do this. Somehow. Because if her answer was no, the deposit on the venue was null and void. All the money she'd already spent on repairs would have to come from somewhere else.

"Do we need to pick up these supplies?" Mason asked.

Both Trish and Lina glanced curiously between Mason and Holly with a look that suggested from the images in their minds, they were up to no good.

"I've hired Mason to help with the barn while he's staying here. That would include this next assignment, too." There, that sounded professional. Not at all like they were a couple or anything.

"Splendid!"

Trish handed Holly a folded purple sticky note. "Tell me if that number will suffice for your trouble. I know this request probably comes at a bad time. So close to the deadline, and I know you have a ranch to run. But my fans have their hearts set on this gala. I can't let them down at the last minute."

Holly honestly wasn't sure what a fair number would be. It wasn't something she'd ever considered. She could manage a ranch, assign duties, move and vaccinate the herd with the best of them. Even help keep watch for a wolf that threatened their livelihood. But event planning?

"That should be more than enough," Lina added when Holly had yet to unfold the Post-It note.

Holly bent back the corner of the paper for a quick peek.

Five thousand dollars?

"I think you added an extra zero." She handed the note back, but Trish refused to take it.

"No, that's what I'm offering. This event is very special to me. Special to my readers, too. I've promised to live stream it to my followers on social media. I may have already mentioned it in my last newsletter to see what they thought, and the response was unbelievable. I *need* this event to happen."

The details raced through Holly's mind. One ranch hand off the rest of the week. Another off until January, starting tomorrow. They were shorthanded, and the cattle didn't care whether there was a Christmas gala or not. The wolf would certainly like her odds better, too.

"I'm around to help," Mason said.

"It's a lot of money, Trish." *The ranch can use the income.* Already, Holly could assign every dollar. "Are you sure?"

"I have no doubt you'll earn every penny." When Holly still failed to relent, Trish added, "You won't get the bonus until the event is over. Does that make it seem more fair? Please say you'll do this."

Before Holly could summon a list of reasons to turn this down, she said, "Done."

Trish threw her arms around Holly's neck and squeezed her tight. "Thank you, thank you! You have no idea how much this means to me."

Lina patted Holly on the arm as they walked toward the door. "We really appreciate this. More than you know." She looked at Mason. "Can you swing by the ranch later today and pick up some decorations? We could only fit a few totes today."

He nodded. "I'll be right out to grab those."

Hope bubbled in Holly's chest at what Mason sticking around to help might mean. "Are you staying through Christmas Eve, then?" She pushed away any silly fantasies of attending the gala with him. They'd be working that night, no doubt.

Leaving her with a wink at the door, he said, "Guess I am."

CHAPTER 10

Mason

"What are we doing?" Holly asked when Mason turned into town instead of toward the gravel road to the ranch. The truck was filled to the brim with Christmas decorations Lina and the rest of the book club ladies had rounded up. Blitzen poked his head out from the back seat, the loose branches of a Christmas tree dangling above his perked ears.

"We're getting groceries."

Holly folded her hands in her lap. "We don't really have time for that. I can order another pizza from Mario's—"

"Or eat a peanut butter and jelly?"

She offered a mild shrug. "It's quicker."

He rolled to a stop at the intersection near the grocery store. Blitzen failed at his attempt to go on high alert from the back seat; the totes of Christmas lights were in his way. So he wriggled until his front paws stood on the center console. With the store only a block away, Mason let him keep his perch.

"I don't know how long you've been living on those sandwiches, but tonight it ends. I'm cooking us dinner."

"You don't have to do that, Mason. You've already done so much—"

"I know I don't, but I'm going to." The truth was, he'd thought about it all day. All night, really, while he drifted in and out of sleep. Holly's smile lived in his dreams, however briefly. Maybe dinner wasn't the best idea with them all alone in the house, but she deserved a break, if only for a short while. Let someone else do something for her. "Plus, Brantley mentioned his mom was getting in tomorrow. Do you want your aunt to starve?"

She held up her hands in surrender. "You win."

Mason teased, "Tough battle I fought."

"What can I say? I'm a sucker for a home-cooked meal. Especially one *I* don't have to make."

"I'd ask for requests, but I'm surprising you." He parked the truck, about to pull the key out of the ignition, but then thought better of it. "Why don't you wait here? Keep Blitzen from busting up all the decorations? I won't be long."

"Let me give you some m—"

Mason hopped out of the truck before she could fulfill that offer. The last thing he'd do was take money from a Maxwell. They'd always been so generous to him. Making a couple of meals was the least he could do.

He gave up cradling ingredients in his arms five items in, returning to the front to snag a cart. He'd no more than freed himself of groceries before he heard his name.

"Mason Montgomery, in the flesh. If I didn't see it with my own eyes, I never would've believed it was true." Amelia West threw her arms around him seconds before he set the package of steaks in his cart. "You're home."

He hugged her tight, letting her rock them in that motherly way she always had with him. "When did you sneak into town?" he asked.

She pulled back from him, adjusting the strap on her purse that'd slipped in their embrace. "About twenty minutes ago." Amelia picked up a basket of groceries she'd set on the floor. "Don't tell Brantley. That kid really loves driving to the airport. I don't want to break his heart until I absolutely have to." A twinkle danced in her eyes, reminding him how much he used to enjoy having her in his life. She'd always been there when he needed her, always lightened the mood when things grew grim. They'd talked a lot less since Paul passed away, almost three years ago.

"You want to join us for dinner?" he offered.

Amelia peered into his cart, giving an approving nod at the haul he'd procured from the meat counter. "I have yet in my life to turn down a good steak."

Mason supposed he'd better grab a couple more. Hopes to get Holly's secret from its lock-and-key hold via an intimate dinner he'd planned were diminishing, but the company was a fair trade. "Good. I'll be putting them on the grill in an hour."

"How have you been, Mason? I hear you're in the Special Forces now. Where does the army have you these days? Anyone special in your life?"

The swift onslaught of questions made his head spin, and suddenly he wanted nothing more than to leave the store. Return to his quiet hideaway on the ranch. Or hop on a plane and get himself back to North Carolina. "Holly's waiting in the truck," he said in an attempt to avoid answering questions for as long as possible. But when Amelia's eyes lit up with misunderstanding, he immediately added, "She hired me to help out with some things on the ranch. Keeping me busy so I don't go crazy."

"Ah." But her smile didn't fade, leaving Mason to worry about jumped conclusions.

"You have a ride out there?"

"Drove myself."

"From Arizona?"

Amelia shrugged. "Had to give a friend a ride."

"Are all the Wests still as stubborn as I remember?" Mason teased, eyes catching sight of Holly in the truck through the storefront window. Blitzen stood with all fours on the center console now. If he took much longer, Holly might feel the need to come in. It might delay them.

"It's so good to have you home, Mason. I hope you're staying through Christmas."

"I am." The decision had only been made this morning, and it still felt a little uncomfortable. He itched to return to base, to get that signature so he could get those orders. But the urgency he felt on his first day back in Starlight wasn't as strong now. Maybe he could try relaxing for a few days, as the doc suggested.

"Good, I'm so glad to hear it." Amelia patted his arm with her slender fingers. "I'll see you back at the house."

He quickly gathered the remaining ingredients, thankful there wasn't a line at the checkout counter.

"How is it possible that you haven't put up the Christmas tree yet?" Amelia asked while cutting into her New York strip that night. "If Grandma Charlotte knew it wasn't decorated already, she'd have a cow!"

Holly ducked her head, pushing green beans around on her plate instead of eating them. Sometimes, Mason noted, she took things much too closely to heart. "I haven't—"

"We were planning to put that up tonight, actually," he said. It'd give him an opportunity to uncover that secret Holly was keeping, since the dinner would no longer do. "Can't remember the last time I decorated a tree, to be honest. Kind of looking forward to it."

"Well then, it's a good thing you came home for Christmas this year," Amelia said, approval in her tone. "I'll leave you two to handle that. I have to deliver a gift to an old friend. Going to stay in town tonight, but I'll be back first thing in the morning."

Mason couldn't imagine anyone wanting to drive another mile after the long trek she had, but Amelia West was a determined woman. "Anyone I know?" he asked casually. But the quick blush to her cheeks warned him he asked the wrong question.

"Am I in my old room?" Amelia asked Holly, dropping silverware onto her empty plate. Seemed everything, to include his special baked bean recipe, was a hit with her. "The one across the hall from you?"

"Yep, it is." Holly finally ate a few pieces of steak. "This is wonderful, Mason. You've been holding out on me."

Amelia's gaze danced between the two. "Just how long have you been home, Mason?"

It was his turn to feel some level of embarrassment. He'd been a perfect gentleman, and nothing inappropriate had transpired between him and Holly. He'd almost kissed her that night in the office as he wiped away tears. But *almost* didn't count. Though he found himself quite fond of her, he couldn't imagine anyone in the Maxwell family—namely Lawrence—approving.

"Couple weeks," he answered cautiously. Even if Lawrence's rule wasn't hanging over him, there were still too many complications. He'd be leaving soon. And Holly would never abandon the ranch to come with him. He knew that. "We've been cleaning out that old barn. Did you tell her about the Christmas Eve dance?"

"Dance?" Amelia repeated.

He finished his meal leisurely as Holly filled her aunt in with the details. "I thought it might be a good source of future revenue." Always the businesswoman, he noted, listening. "But I don't want to be the event coordinator next time. I'd rather hire someone else. I have the decorating sense of a cardboard box."

Mason was sure she was exaggerating, and almost said as much. But Amelia didn't give him the chance.

"What does your grandfather think of this holiday dance?"

Eyes glued to her plate, Holly said, "I may not have mentioned it to him yet."

Even Mason felt a jolt of shock at that admission. Though Holly was managing the ranch and was fully capable of making decisions, he'd never have guessed that she'd keep this a secret from Lawrence.

"You might consider telling him. Soon." Amelia dabbed the corners of her lips with a napkin and dropped it onto her empty plate. "Mason, that was absolutely delicious. I can't remember the last time I had a real steak, cooked just the way I like it."

"Happy you could join us." He hoped the line of questioning would hold off until tomorrow. Amelia was the only one who seemed to know anything about the Special Forces, and, well, he didn't really want to get into it. Holly would want him to explain, and that would lead too closely to the truth he was desperate to hide. "How's Arizona been?"

"Wonderful!" Halfway into dessert, Amelia gushed about the weather, the outdoor life she was enjoying on a regular basis, and the multiple trips she'd taken to the Grand Canyon. "Would you believe that in some places, cattle roam free? They have signs up, like they would for deer here, to warn you."

"Wonder if any of those cows want to move to Wyoming?" Holly mumbled. Mason studied her from his side of the table, pondering whether she meant for anyone else to hear that comment.

"Think Norbert could use a friend?" he dared.

"Norbert?" Amelia repeated.

Holly shot him an incredulous look, but Mason held steadfast. This was simply practice for much more difficult conversations ahead. Surely she could appreciate that. Besides, he'd be shocked if Amelia hadn't yet noticed the calf lingering on the porch. Norbert had been pushing the red ball around with his nose when they pulled up, waiting for his best friend to return. "The calf Holly saved this spring."

"Uh oh, you named him."

"I know, I know." Holly gathered the plates from the table and took them to the kitchen sink to rinse off. The task turned extra noisy, and Amelia gave Mason a questioning look.

"I didn't know it was a secret," he said to Amelia, doubtful Holly could hear him over the clatter of dishes and running water. "I'm sure you've seen him?"

"I've got to update some ledgers," Holly told them once the water stopped. She hastily dried her hands, balling up the towel and tossing it on the counter when she finished. "I'll be in my office if you need me."

Mason unsuccessfully hid his frown, otherwise Amelia wouldn't have questioned it.

"Something going on between you two I should

know about?" At least she waited to ask until the latch clicked, barricading Holly inside her office.

"No." The answer was immediate, assured. But inside, Mason felt a little despondent. The feeling was new. "Just helping her out with a few things, like I said."

Amelia pushed back in her chair. "Could've fooled me."

In the army, Mason had been so careful to keep a guard around his heart all these years. He traveled too much. Spent too much time on critical missions he couldn't tell anyone about. Faced dangers that would give most people nightmares. Adding someone else in the mix . . .

Amelia patted him on the arm on her way to the door. "Christmas decorations are in the crawlspace in the back of the house. There's a door near yours. Hope you didn't have any other plans tonight."

CHAPTER 11

Holly

She'd tried to start it over at least three times, but inside she was fuming. Despite her best effort, Holly couldn't focus on the list in front of her. What right did Mason have to tell Amelia about Norbert? Holly'd been upset about the Christmas Eve dance at first too, but her aunt would figure that out on her own. With the book club on the loose, surely the entire town already knew.

Blitzen wasn't a fan of her pacing, and with it getting so close to dark, he was worried about his best friend. He whined and looked at the door she rarely closed.

With great reluctance, Holly abandoned her

sanctuary and bravely stepped out into the hallway. "Let's go check on Norbert." Her dog zipped around her, nearly buckling her legs with his pushiness. The way he cared about his best friend touched her heart, though, so she was hardly upset.

What am I going to do?

Once her grandpa learned about Norbert sleeping on the back porch and eating his dinner outside the kitchen window, he'd put an instant stop to all of it. And Holly didn't know how to keep that from happening.

She refilled the heated water dish. Next, she adjusted Norbert's bed, a combination of hay and Blitzen's old flannel puppy blanket that he'd decorated with a few bite marks. Blitzen watched from the window as Norbert curled up in his spot sheltered from the wind.

"Sleep tight, Norbert." Holly hardly closed the door before Mason startled her.

"Is there a key for that crawlspace door?"

It took her a moment to place what he was asking. "Key." *The Christmas tree.* "Yeah, let me grab it." She refused to meet his eyes as she passed him, headed toward her office. Surely she'd cave if that happened, and right now, she wanted to be upset with him. What if Aunt Amelia told her grandparents about Norbert before they got home? Her grandpa's mind was the hardest to sway if he'd already made it up.

"How big's this tree anyway?" Mason asked as she dug around in a desk drawer.

The crawlspace was packed to the brim with decorations, and once they managed to get everything returned to its home last Christmas, Holly wasn't eager to repeat the process.

"Huge."

"I'm guessing Christmas hasn't changed much around here, then?"

Christmas was less than a week away, and guilt tugged at her. There hadn't been a holiday season in her entire childhood that the decorations still lay tucked away in the crawlspace come December first. Grandma Charlotte would be disappointed to say the least. *One more thing for the list.*

"I'm not sure what'll be a bigger chore—decorating the barn or decorating the house." She handed him the key, annoyed that the heat of their light graze sent tingles up her arm. Maybe it was a good thing they could never be a couple. Holly would never be able to stay mad at him for more than a few minutes.

"I'll get everything down to the living room," he said, eyes scanning the mess of ledgers and crumpled paper scattered on her desk. "Meet me there in half an hour?"

Holly would've helped him, and Grandpa would've scolded her now to see her, but she needed some time.

Time to figure out how she was going to pay for

the new heating unit that'd been installed in the writer's cabin today. Time to skim even a couple of chapters so she wouldn't have to rely solely on Mason's expertise when it came to decorating the barn. Time to remind herself that after Christmas, he'd leave. He'd go back to his job in the army, and there was no guarantee he'd ever come back.

Blitzen, however, was more than happy to label himself a traitor. He trotted after Mason, intrigued by this turn of events. "Thanks," she muttered.

Holly closed the door behind them, determined to find the answers to her dilemmas in this quiet half hour. Her grandpa had told her one of her strengths was making the best of a bad situation. At the very least, she could clean up her messy desk. Grandpa would disapprove of that most of all.

Before she could scribble a single word on her list of things to do before her grandparents made it home, a gentle knock sounded at her door. The click-clack on the hardwood gave them both away. She let out a defeated sigh. No way he was done already. "Come in."

"I might need your help with the tree," Mason said. "It's a little taller than I remembered. Kind of awkward to carry. Wondering if you hold the secret to getting it down a spiral staircase."

"Right." Holly pushed out of her chair, following the pair upstairs to the crawlspace entrance.

"After this tree, I think I can get the rest," Mason

said, almost in apology, when they reached the top of the stairs. "I know you have a lot to do."

But she was too preoccupied by the cracked door that revealed a meticulously clean room, the comforter tucked in at sharp angles. A pair of combat boots sat neatly lined up at the foot of the bed. "I can help," she finally said.

Something colorful caught her eye from beneath the bed, oddly out of place in the otherwise spotless room. "Is that my missing reindeer sock?" But before she investigated, Mason was shoving a tree her way.

"Could you grab the top?"

Grandma Charlotte's artificial tree had been in the family for years. Though it used to come apart in sections, Grandpa and Bobby had welded them together a number of years ago to protect the integrity of the stem. An idea Grandpa deemed brilliant . . . until it came time to put it away.

Holly hugged the top half of the tree, her back to Mason. "I don't even remember the days when this used to come apart."

The branches were smashed flat against the middle, a quilted bag Grandma Charlotte stitched herself wrapped around it like a cocoon. It would take over an hour to shape the branches alone. But that task was nonnegotiable, and necessary to complete to perfection.

"I've seen more Christmas decorations today than I have in probably ten years," Mason mentioned as they slowly descended the stairs. "Almost forgot how much some people love this holiday."

Something about that admission softened Holly's resolve to stay mad at him about outing Norbert to Aunt Amelia. "You don't decorate for Christmas?" It was a loaded question, and she had no idea what to expect in answer.

"Not ever in one place very long."

The words struck her as odd. He'd stayed in Alaska six years. That seemed long in military terms. She remembered Paul complaining about that years ago when he'd been hopeful about staying at Fort Wainwright. But because the army denied him that opportunity, wanting him to move after only three years, he opted to let his enlistment period expire after the deployment.

"Does that mean you don't even put up a tree?"

Finally, they were on the ground floor. How they'd maneuvered that tall tree around the spiral staircase, Holly wasn't sure. It was a magic trick every year, and no one seemed to capture the secret behind it.

"Don't see a point."

"So, you *are* a Scrooge."

His eyes widened at her teasing, forcing her to look away. *I'm* not *flirting with Mason!* Any notion she'd had about the two of them, well, it was gone. He'd leave in a little over a week. *Maybe sooner.*

"I have things I like about Christmas."

"Oh, really?" She couldn't resist. "Like what?"

"I like eggnog."

Holly laughed, quite loudly judging by Blitzen joining in and barking along with her. His tail wagged as he tried to figure out if there was a game to be played. "That's not exactly what I meant."

"Christmas ham?"

They both laughed this time as they set the tree down. Together, they released the Velcroed straps and carefully unwrapped the quilted cover. "Surely you associate more than food with Christmas?"

"But the food is *so* good."

After the tree stood upright and level, Mason left Holly to shape branches while he retrieved the rest of the decorations. She wished she had some treat to share with him tonight, even microwave popcorn. It would be a chore to get this tree to Grandma Charlotte's standard. The branches were long, full, and plentiful. The decorations too numerous to count.

"I have a new appreciation for the Maxwell family." Mason set down a tower of three totes filled with Christmas lights. "I never got in on the *bringing boxes downstairs* bit of your family Christmas. I only showed up to reap the benefits. Eat the food, watch the movie, open presents."

Holly's cheeks heated almost on cue, forcing her to turn away so she wouldn't have to explain the memory. That Christmas when she was fourteen—the last Christmas Mason spent with them until this one—she had the worst crush on him. She'd hung on his every word. Wrote her name in her notebook as Mrs. Holly Montgomery. She'd been too nervous to sit by him on the couch during the family movie, though he offered her a spot.

Mason set off down the hallway. "I'll be back."

Blitzen paused near the couch, debating whether to follow Mason to the far corner of the house again or stay with Holly. "I'm fresh out of treats," she told the dog. As if he understood, he trotted off after Mason.

When Mason returned, she had most of the branches pulled away from the center. And a solid ten percent of them shaped when she turned to find him with another stack of totes filled with more Christmas lights. Mason looked at her from over the armful. "These can't all be for this one tree."

"Some are for outside." *Another thing to add to the list.* She had no clue when they'd find time to hang lights with how short-staffed they'd be from now until Christmas. She had already assigned her hands more chores than was fair. And tomorrow she'd be checking and repairing fences herself.

"That's something I like."

"What?"

"About Christmas." Mason stepped toward the tree to shape branches alongside Holly. "I used to drive around with my parents—or at least whichever one was home for Christmas. Half the time, one of them was deployed. But no matter what was happening, we always found one night to drive around and look at Christmas lights. I miss it."

Holly's heart melted a bit at that admission. He'd rarely talked about his parents when he worked on the ranch, the sting of losing them too fresh. She'd always wanted to know more about them, but the opportunity to ask never presented itself back then. "Do you still go? To look at lights?"

Scrubbing a hand through his hair, he answered, "Nah. Haven't in years." He shuffled away from the tree, off for another load of decorations, no doubt. Her gaze trailed after him, and if she wasn't mistaken, he was limping a little on one leg. *What's that about?*

Taking a break from shaping branches that made her hands ache, Holly went in search of a notepad. This one listed the Christmas things to be done prior to her grandparents' arrival. Even if her grandpa decided she wasn't fit to run the ranch anymore, at least she could deliver the Christmas they were accustomed to. Well, plus a barn filled with people on Christmas Eve.

Back in the living room, she jotted down everything that came to mind.

Decorate tree.

Hang stockings.

Switch out wall hangings.

Hang outdoor lights.

Set up inflatable reindeer.

Holly paused at the last one, wondering what Norbert would think of his air-filled friends. She let out a chuckle, imagining him sniffing one like a dog.

"You want to start decorating the barn tomorrow?" Mason asked, dropping off more totes. From a glance, Holly thought she spotted snowmen.

Set up snowmen collection.

"I'm hoping we have time to set up trees. Start hanging lights." Most of the decorations would need to wait until the event was closer, but the sooner they tackled the things they could do easily, the less sleep they'd lose later. "I have a list."

Mason chuckled. "Let me guess. For things to do now, and another list for things to do right before?"

Seemed she blushed a lot around Mason these days, she realized. *Bad. This is very bad.* "Yes."

"What list are you on now?"

She handed Mason her pad of paper. "When do you sleep?"

"December twenty-sixth!" They laughed over it, something they did quite often, it seemed. This lighter side to Mason Montgomery was one she rarely experienced as a teenager. She found she liked it, maybe a little too much. "I should tell Brantley I'm not working at all that day. I'm just going to sleep."

"Might not be a terrible idea."

Holly shook her head, dismissing it as easily as it came up. "No, the animals don't care if you're tired.

They still need feeding, watering, looking after." That they had a possible wolf on the prowl reminded her to follow up with her cousin tomorrow, see if they made any progress tracking it down.

"I get it." Mason took a seat on the couch near an outlet to unravel lights, plugging in a strand to test it. "Overseas it's definitely like that. They can't tell you to forget the reason you're over there fighting for one day because it's a holiday or you're too tired. The enemy doesn't care if it's Christmas or if you really want a two-day nap."

She wanted to ask more, because her gut told her Mason was holding back quite a lot. "How many times have you gone over there?"

"A few."

Returning to shaping branches, Holly couldn't shake the evasive answer that only raised more flags. She wanted to believe he was being modest, but that wasn't it. She'd bet the ranch on it.

CHAPTER 12

Mason

Mason awoke with a crick in his neck. He blinked away disorientation. *Where am I?* It took him a few moments to realize the colorful glowing lights were strung on a Christmas tree in the Maxwells' living room.

He kicked his feet to the floor, wiping sleep from his eyes. *The couch.* He'd fallen asleep on the couch. It came back to him in pieces, Holly shaping branches, himself testing lights. Them both sitting down to take a 'quick' break that seemed to have resulted in a long snooze.

Holly lay curled up on the couch's opposite end,

her right arm poking out from under a small throw blanket. Blitzen curled at her feet. How long had they been asleep? Standing in search of a clock, he debated whether to let her sleep or wake her so she could go to bed.

The dog sleepily opened his eyes, but Blitzen didn't budge from his comfy spot. *I'll let her stay.* Mason gently tugged the blanket to cover her exposed shoulder. She nestled further into the throw pillow. She looked so peaceful sleeping there. He had forgotten what sleep like that felt like.

The clock on the kitchen stove read two fifty-nine. *Three hours?* Mason tried to remember when they took a break, but all he knew was that it was before midnight.

He trudged upstairs and dropped onto his bed, hopeful that tonight he might actually sleep. He didn't care what the reason was behind it, whether it was the number of tasks he'd piled on, or that his body was too tired to keep up this charade of insomnia. He didn't care. Tonight, he finally felt a shred of hope.

Thrilled at the prospect of eating a real breakfast—and though the donuts from Millie's Bakery were quite tasty, he'd grown tired of them—the next morning Mason whipped up scrambled eggs, bacon, and waffles for them. In total, he was certain he'd stolen four and a half hours of solid sleep. It felt like twenty.

All he could think about since the moment he peeled himself off the couch was calling his commanding officer. Telling him he finally slept more than an hour.

"If I had known you were this good at cooking, I would've hired you to feed me instead." Holly poured herself a cup of coffee, stirring in some of the caramel creamer he'd picked up at the store yesterday.

The closing front door drew both of their attention for a moment.

"It's nice to have time to cook." He scolded himself for waiting so long to get groceries. That'd been his original objective for fixing up the old truck. But the stubborn thing had already broken down within the property lines of the ranch twice, and he wasn't sure he'd have another opportunity to tinker with it.

"Do I smell bacon?" Amelia unwrapped a scarf from her neck, greeting them with a cheerful smile. For a woman who'd driven a little over a thousand miles this week, she looked remarkably refreshed.

"Now, what's breakfast without bacon?" Mason replied.

Holly was halfway through an adorable yawn—

fault of the Christmas tree and the never-ending branches that needed shaping—when Amelia stopped them both. "This Christmas Eve dance you mentioned. The one in the barn. Word is *all* over town."

Mason watched the exchange between Amelia and Holly over his shoulder as he continued to scramble the eggs.

"That'll be the Starlight Book Club at work." Holly stirred something in her coffee, or maybe she just needed to fiddle with the spoon. "Sounds like it's going to be a big event."

Amelia slipped into a chair a second before Blitzen rushed over to greet her. "And you don't think you should mention this to your grandparents?"

What Mason wouldn't give to know what secrets Holly Maxwell was guarding. There was more than fear of her grandpa's disapproval lingering there. Far as he knew, they had a carefully calculated budget to adhere to for fixing up the barn, and they'd come in under.

"I'll give them a call today." Holly's gaze was pointed down at her cup of coffee. "It all happened so fast."

As Mason plated three portions of eggs, Amelia draped an arm around Holly's shoulder and pulled her in for a hug. "I'm not trying to be harsh on you, kiddo. I know he left you in charge. But this is *not* something he'd want to find out through town gossip. Trust me on that."

"I know."

"Can't really make a great suggestion about the cow," Amelia added, looking out the kitchen window at the black calf staring in. Blitzen's tail wagged, but he wasn't about to abandon the hand scratching behind his ears. "But he sure is cute. I'm sure you'll think of something."

"You sure you're up for helping with chores today?" Holly asked Mason after they finished breakfast, giving him the chance to stay behind.

He almost took it, to make that call. But it wouldn't change anything. The doc still had to clear him, and four hours of sleep broken into two chunks during one night wouldn't convince anyone to sign those papers allowing him to return to his unit and get back to the missions. "Yeah, let's get to it." Besides, spending a little time with Holly sounded a lot more appealing than hiding out in the house all day.

"It's going to be a long day."

"What's up first?"

"Quick huddle with the crew. Then you and I'll be checking fences."

Mundane task for sure, he remembered well. He

did that weekly the last summer he worked here. At least he wouldn't be sweating incessantly from the beating sun and hot summer air. "Got everything we need?"

"Almost." Holly left him at the door to button up his coat, returning with a rifle. A Winchester 243, if his first glance was correct. Perfect for predators like coyotes or wolves. *Impressive.* "We'll need to keep a lookout for tracks, too. No one has found the wolf yet."

Mason couldn't quite catch his breath. Holly looked so brave. Fierce. Something threatened her ranch, and she wasn't afraid to do what was necessary to protect it. It was quite possible he was developing real feelings. Caring about someone in a way he never allowed himself before.

"I just need a minute to wrangle Blitzen. He loves riding in the ATV, but today he'll need boots."

"Boots?"

Holly set the rifle in the corner by the door and called the dog over. She commanded him to sit and went in for the first fleece bootie. Blitzen tugged his paw away. "Blitz, c'mon. You can't come with us without these. You're too spoiled with your indoor luxuries for that." With great reluctance, Blitzen relented. But only for the first bootie.

Once secured, he hopped to his feet and limped around on three paws, is if his covered paw were broken.

Mason chuckled at the pitiful demonstration. "Dramatic dog."

"You have no idea." She captured him long enough to slip a second bootie on the opposite back leg. Blitzen didn't appear to know how to walk after that. He tried to limp on both covered paws. The result landed him on his butt. Holly tried to hide her laughter behind her hand, but failed. Blitzen gave Mason the most pathetic look in existence.

"Let me help." He held Blitzen until all the booties were secured and fastened, despite the plea the dog made with a lick to Mason's hand to free him before it was over. "Sorry bud, it's for your own good."

When Blitzen finally managed to get onto all fours, he avoided the hardwood floors, sticking to the edges of the rugs. He walked as if each paw were sticky and had to be peeled from a Velcro floor. "Don't let him fool you. He'll be just fine once he's outside. It'll be like this little episode never happened." Holly zipped up her coat, secured a green scarf that complemented her chocolate eyes, and reached for her Winchester. "Ready?"

"Yeah." Mason couldn't look at her, for fear he'd fall. The kid he'd known more than ten years ago had grown into quite the profound woman.

As she drove her truck to the stable, he again felt the urge to call his commander. It might be time to jet before anything as serious as feelings got involved.

With his line of work, he couldn't afford to get close to anyone. As a boy, he watched his mother cry herself to sleep when his dad was overseas. If she, a soldier too, missed him that much . . . Mason could never ask that of another person. He was gone far more than his parents ever were.

They took Holly's truck as the old Ford wasn't running well. They didn't have time for the unreliable beast to break down and force them to walk. Blitzen paced in the back seat, nosing up the windows Holly refused to open. "It's colder than it looks out there, bud."

When they pulled up, Mason counted three other trucks already parked. It'd been over a decade since he was in this particular stable, waiting for his daily brief and assignments. "Still do this huddle, huh?"

"Why fix something that's not broken?" Holly quoted her grandpa. "Though I will admit, I didn't make too many appearances last week. Just left Brantley to divvy out the task list."

"Did the ranch fall apart?" he asked, recognizing a graveness to her tone that suggested she felt she'd fallen short. Truth was, he wasn't sure how she juggled everything. It made him admire her all the more.

"No, it didn't. As Jillian has reminded me more than once, Brantley is more than capable of running the show when needed." Holly unbuckled her seat belt. "Of course, she thinks I need a vacation and doesn't believe I'll ever take one."

Vacation. The concept sounded foreign to Mason. Outside of this trip to Starlight for the holidays, he hadn't done anything in years that could be considered a vacation. Maybe since his parents died.

"You're frowning."

"Just thinking." He bolted from the truck before she could press further. His life didn't allow for things like R and R. He had a duty to protect his country. It was a choice and a sacrifice he made willingly. Vacations didn't exactly fit into the mix. Until relaxation had been forced on him, he never even considered slowing down. *Stupid leg.*

He followed Holly and an eager Blitzen inside the stable, where a few ranch hands were already gathered, Brantley, Bobby, and a couple of new guys he didn't know. Felt like a small crew for a ranch this size.

"We've got our work cut out for us this week, being down a couple of hands," Holly started. "Any updates, concerns?"

"Heater is up and running in that cabin," Bobby said. He rattled off some details that Holly jotted into her notepad. Her brows furrowed at the price tag, but she didn't comment. Just sucked in a discreet breath no one else but Mason seemed to notice, and kept on writing.

"Is our guest happy?"

"Yes. I offered her that discount you mentioned, and she took it."

"Any updates on the wolf?"

Brantley offered a few details about the last place they spotted tracks, but that was all anyone could tell them. Mason wasn't foolish enough to presume the predator had lost interest in the livestock.

Holly delegated assignments, much as Lawrence used to. The hands, all men but one, listened to what she said, and no one complained about their increased task load. Not even Bobby, forced to muck out stalls, because the newbie they hired to take care of the stables was out for the holidays. "I promise, we'll take turns on that one." The group laughed at that, and someone made a joke about Bobby getting stuck with it until New Year's.

"You're on tomorrow." Holly gave the jokester a wink, earning another round of laughter.

Something uncomfortable twisted in Mason's stomach at that gesture. Or maybe it was the way that ranch hand smiled at Holly after her wink. *I can't be* jealous? That was ridiculous. To be jealous meant . . . He shook the thought away before it could fully manifest.

The group dispersed, and Holly whistled for Blitzen. He was nose-to-nose with a mare at the end of the stable, tail wagging. *Both* tails if his eyes weren't deceiving him. Blitzen, as crazy and reckless as that dog could be, seemed to make friends with all the animals. "Ready to get going?"

He tossed one more suspicious look at the ranch hand who smiled at Holly. Seemed—despite his best reasoning—he was eager to check fences with Holly. "Yeah, let's go."

CHAPTER 13

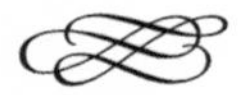

Holly

"You've been spending an awful lot of time with Mason these days," Jillian accused. "Sure there isn't something you want to tell me? You know, your *best friend*?"

"There's nothing to tell." Holly slowly paced the floor of the former ranch hand cabin that they agreed Jillian could convert into a photography studio. This time last year, she was working off her rent in horse chores. Now her talented best friend was much too busy, and paid her rent in the form of a check. Holly's grandpa would no doubt be underwhelmed by the dollar amount they negotiated, but Jillian was practically family.

"I don't believe you."

"Anyway, back to my original question," Holly said. "Do you have any nutcrackers?"

"Finally caught up on reading, are you?"

"I've gotten a few chapters in." That 'few' translated to four; Holly didn't offer up that detail. Without Mason's help, she'd have no idea that every single tree—all twelve—needed its own nutcracker. Grandma Charlotte didn't have a single one in her vast Christmas collection, and so far the book club ladies had only been able to scrounge up one among the group.

"I might have one."

"One." They needed a dozen. Seemed Trish and Lina only had one to offer between the two of them as well. "That leaves me nine more to find." Holly dropped into the only cushy chair in the cabin, distracting herself with the lovely prints on the walls. She remembered a time when those walls were bare.

"You sure there's nothing going on with Mason?" The question came out in almost a whine.

"Why does everyone seem to think that?" But the truth was, Holly had been wondering the same thing.

There were times he looked at her as though he might really *see* her. The way he smiled, the way the lines at the edges of his eyes crinkled when he laughed with her. It didn't help that a single soft touch sent shivers throughout her body for an entire day. She got one now, just thinking about their hands grazing.

"You're blushing."

Jillian was up from her seat at the computer, and much too close for comfort. Lately, Holly's emotions were written all over her face, and she wasn't doing so well at hiding them. Jillian knew her better than anyone. "I don't know what's happening," Holly finally relented. "It's probably all in my head. Like when I was fourteen and foolish."

"What if it's not?"

She hadn't even allowed herself to consider that possibility. Besides, they weren't kids anymore, and Mason would leave soon. He had a commitment, and it didn't sound as if he'd be discharged from the army anytime soon.

She had a ranch to manage—at least, she hoped she was still the manager once Grandpa got back. Even if she was demoted to stable mucker, this was home. She couldn't imagine leaving Starlight behind.

"Can I come by later for that nutcracker?"

"Sure. Stop by the cabin. I'll warn you, though," Jillian added. "It's still in a box. I haven't had much time to decorate, beyond the tree."

The tree! They'd hardly gotten the lights on the tree last night once the branches were shaped. One look at the evergreen this morning warned Holly she had touch-ups to make. Grandma Charlotte would never approve of a sub-satisfactorily shaped tree. "Great, I'll come by after dinner."

"Holly?" Jillian said before she could flee out the door.

"Yeah?"

"Things don't just happen by coincidence, you know."

"What do you mean?" But she had a nagging feeling she knew where this was going.

"Mason shows up the *day* you agree to clean out a massive old barn and host a party in it but have no idea how you're going to accomplish such a major job? That's not a coincidence."

If only Jillian knew how many other things aligned when Mason showed up, Holly would never hear the end of it.

"You two get that tree finished up," Amelia ordered that evening from her post in the kitchen. She'd found one of Grandma Charlotte's aprons decked out with daisies, and had it tied around her waist. "I've got dinner covered."

Mason walked in a few steps behind Holly, tousling his hair and shaking out the flatness from a stocking cap. After her stop at Jillian's cabin, Holly had picked him up from the stables so they could check on the barn and unload another batch of decorations. "No hints?" he asked.

Briefly, she tried to picture what he'd look like in a Stetson. He'd worn one often years ago, in the warmer months. But now that he was older . . .

"Shoo! Both of you!" Amelia waved a spatula at them, any attempt to peek at the dinner preparations intercepted. "I'll call you when it's ready."

Holly skittered down the hall toward the explosion of Christmas decorations they had to leave behind this morning in exchange for a full day's worth of chores. Outside of dropping off more things, they hadn't even had a chance to put up any of the barn decorations. "You don't have to tell me twice!" said Holly.

"Whatever it is, it smells amazing." Mason's stomach growled on cue. They'd spent a grueling day, riding along the fence lines, making several repairs, and searching for nonexistent wolf tracks. Other than a couple of peanut butter and jelly sandwiches, they hadn't eaten much since breakfast.

"I'm going to get too spoiled over the holidays," she told Mason as they arrived in the living room to tackle garland and ornaments. The other stacks of odd decorations and outdoor lights would have to wait for another day. She really needed to call Grandma Charlotte. "These home-cooked meals are making me wish I could hire a chef."

"You don't like to cook?" Mason asked as he

sifted through a tote of garland, separating silver from red.

"It's not my favorite thing," she admitted.

"Not high on the list, then?" A twinkle flashed in his eyes, making her once again wonder whether he was flirting or just comfortable around her now that they'd spent so much time together.

"Not high on *any* list." Holly searched for a shoebox filled with ornament hooks. Grandma Charlotte was strict about saving every single one each year, and if her claims were true, she hadn't spent a dime on them in over a decade. "I'd happily survive on PB and Js and coffee if it meant I never had to cook."

"Don't forget Millie's Bakery." He was teasing again; she was sure of it.

"I have to call my grandma. I'm long overdue. Think you can hold down the fort for a few minutes?"

"You going to tell her about the dance?"

Reluctantly, Holly said, "That's the plan." She imagined her grandma would be tickled at such a fun idea, and if it came to life anything like the author dreamed up, it would be amazing. But her grandpa might not feel so warm and fuzzy about such a project that obviously stole time from a struggling ranch.

In her office, Holly closed the door and steadied

herself with a few deep breaths. Then she dialed her grandma's number.

"Holly! What a pleasant surprise!" Grandma Charlotte was one of the most cheerful people she'd ever known, and hearing her voice after several weeks was refreshing. Like drinking from a cold spring after a long day in the sun, working on the ranch.

"Hi, Grandma Charlotte. How are things?"

"We're still in Florida, dear. We just love it here!" The light roar of people chatting filtered through the phone. "So sunny, and the beach is beautiful. We have this fabulous little place we visit for breakfast every morning."

"Sounds like a dream."

"It's a little slice of paradise. How are things back at the ranch?"

Holly dropped into her rolling chair and nearly sent herself backwards into a filing cabinet. She abandoned the dangerous contraption and returned to good ol' pacing the room. "Aunt Amelia got in yesterday. She's making sure we don't starve. And Mason's here too this year. He's been helping out around the ranch."

"Mason! Yes, Brantley told me he was coming. It'll be so wonderful to see him." Grandma Charlotte sounded a little distracted. Holly could only guess what she might be up to, but the seagulls crying in the background suggested they were near water.

Avoiding the topic she really needed to discuss, Holly asked another question instead. "Are you ready to head back soon?"

"We'll be packing up in the next couple of days. I sure do miss the snow. Doesn't quite feel like Christmas here, you know?"

A couple of days? Holly did the math in her head, but the drive from Destin to Starlight could take two days or ten, depending on how many detours they made. "You'll be back in time for Christmas though, right?"

"Oh yes, of course. Wouldn't miss it! We'll be there by Christmas morning as planned."

Holly should tell Grandma Charlotte about the Christmas Eve dance, but fear held her back. What if she shared the news with her grandpa and he called back and told her to cancel the whole thing? She'd have to repay Trish the money she already spent and let down the entire community.

The risk of his wrath after the event already happened would surely be better than the alternative. *Right?* And if it was a success—because it had to be—she could appease Grandpa with numbers. He'd appreciate that more.

"I don't want to keep you from enjoying your last days in Florida, and I better get back to it anyway. See you at Christmas, Grandma."

"I can't wait to see how the tree turned out!

Maybe you can send me a picture on your camera phone."

Holly silently chuckled. Her grandma wasn't the most tech savvy, but she was trying to keep up with the latest technologies anyway. "I can send you a picture, though the surprise might be worth the wait."

"Well, whatever you decide."

"Bye, Grandma. Tell Grandpa I send my love."

She hung up before her grandma could think to pass the phone to him. Holly loved her grandpa, and he loved his family very much, but she ran double duty as both granddaughter and manager of the ranch he'd expanded into a powerhouse. She hoped this past dismal year wouldn't put too big a damper on the ranch's reputation.

She felt eager to return to the living room. *To finish the tree*, she told herself. It had nothing to do with Mason. In the doorway, she dared let her eyes fall on him from across the room, and the sight left her in a fit of giggles. He appeared to be quite tangled in a mix of red and silver garland.

"Need some help over there, soldier?" Holly maneuvered around totes and over strings of lights before he could decline. She unwrapped garland draped around his shoulders that had somehow pinned one of his arms. "I can't even guess how this happened."

Mason offered only a shrug. "Blitzen distracted me."

The dog's head tilted at his name, but his attention quickly went back to the bay window. Norbert was munching on a snack in the backyard.

"Sure, blame the dog." She attempted to roll her eyes, but his intense gaze made her breath catch. Her shaky hand grazed his collarbone. She turned away, letting her hair curtain her heated cheeks. She fought to ignore her erratic pulse and hurried with unwinding the garland until Mason was mostly free.

A long curl of her hair tangled in the garland, binding them together. "Hold still," Mason said, his voice calm and collected. She supposed it was only *her* heart ready to beat right out of its chest at their proximity. She felt the gentle tug of her hair as she worked to free it. "There." He tucked the curl behind her ear. "Threat contained."

The smile that escaped at his military jargon wasn't lost on him. He smiled back. *I should look away*, but this close to him, she was entranced. "Thank you."

His eyes dropped to her lips in a flicker. "You're welcome."

Blitzen barked then, causing Holly to jump back. She tripped over a pile of lights and went backwards into the couch. After the beat of embarrassment passed, she laughed. What else could she do? The tense moment dissipated as quickly as it began. *For the best.*

Mason offered his hand. "I think he saw a squirrel. Couldn't let anyone near his best friend, you know." He pulled her to her feet, and she nearly collided with his chest.

"Dinner's ready," Amelia announced from the doorway. "Looks like you two didn't get far at all on that tree."

"Had a little untangling to do," Mason answered, taking a step away from Holly and toward the doorway. She felt his absence immediately, and it left her more confused than ever.

CHAPTER 14

Mason

I almost kissed her. All logic and reasoning he'd kept close had flown out the window, and he nearly kissed Holly. Blitzen's squirrel excitement was the only thing that stopped him. Had it not been for that, Amelia would've witnessed the whole thing, too late to do anything but let Mr. Maxwell know what she saw. And likely what she presumed transpired in the house before her arrival.

"You don't have to worry about the dishes," Amelia told him. "I can wash those up."

"It's no bother." For the first time, fear of exile lingered. If he broke Lawrence Maxwell's one rule—or if the man *thought* he did—Mason might need to find different accommodations. Flying back to base was, for once, the last thing on his mind. He wanted more time.

It was evasive, maybe a little cowardly, to hide in the kitchen while Holly finished the tree. But it was the only thing he could do to get some space. It hadn't even snowed again, so shoveling the walkway was out. And if he started anything in the barn tonight, he had no doubt she'd show up with one of her lists.

Amelia patted him on the shoulder. "I've never been a fan of washing dishes, so I won't argue with you."

He expected her to leave him to his chore, but instead she leaned against the counter next to the sink. "Are you okay, Mason?"

"Of course."

Amelia stretched her neck around the doorway before saying, "It's wonderful to have you home for Christmas, truly it is. And I love you. But why are you here?"

He wasn't prepared for that question. Maybe he'd let his guard down since Amelia hadn't peppered him with questions over dinner the last two evenings. His shoulders went rigid as he prepared as generic an answer as possible. "Missed this place."

The look Amelia gave him made him feel about

two feet tall. She'd always been able to tell when he was lying, better than his grandma ever had.

When she wouldn't drop her stare, he added, "I needed some time off." It was the truth, if only a slice.

"What happened?"

Mason turned to fill the sink with soapy water, but mostly he hoped the faucet's noise would drown out any chance of Holly overhearing. "I got hurt. My leg. Few months back." He wasn't about to provide details. They didn't matter anyway. "It's taking too long to heal."

Amelia folded her arms, an eyebrow raising. "So you thought coming back here and working until you dropped would help speed that along?"

She reminded him of his mom in so many ways. The same stern look when he didn't cough up the whole truth. Too smart to miss illogical pieces of his story. The same gentleness lingering in her eyes despite all that.

"I haven't been sleeping well."

"Insomnia?"

Leave it to Amelia to nail it on her first guess. "Yeah."

"Any progress?"

"Finally slept a few hours last night, actually." Most people wouldn't celebrate four hours of sleep, but he felt like throwing a parade. "Once I'm able to get a few nights' rest, I'll go back." He didn't need anyone knowing what was riding on that. No need for anyone else to worry about him or extend him pity.

"Does Holly know?"

Forced to turn off the faucet or risk the sink overflowing, he answered, "No." He shook his head. "I'd prefer to keep it that way."

He waited for her to ask *why*, but instead she patted his forearm on her way out of the kitchen, leaving him alone with his whirlwind thoughts and a sink full of dinner dishes. He'd always missed Starlight. His time on this ranch was the best he had after his parents died. He felt at peace here.

Blitzen trotted into the kitchen, poking him with his nose. "Hey, bud."

His tail wagged as Mason scratched him behind the ears one good time before he submerged his hands in water. Maybe one of the reasons Holly didn't care for cooking was the number of dishes it racked up. There was no sign of a dishwasher anywhere.

And there he went again, thinking about Holly.

"What am I going to do, huh?" he asked the dog. But Blitzen merely plopped down at his feet and licked his paws, completely indifferent to Mason's dilemma.

Mason busied himself with the dishes, distracting himself from all thoughts of Holly. But any attempt to replay old missions in his head was lost to the Christmas music coming from down the hall. Seemed Holly wasn't affected at all by what happened, if the upbeat version of "Santa Claus is Coming to Town" had anything to say about that.

He towel-dried his hands, finding himself out of excuses to avoid helping her finish the tree. He'd just be careful to keep free of garland-related tasks.

In the doorway to the living room, he stopped, laughter rocking him. The tree stood decked out in a thick mass of ornaments, but only as high as Holly could reach. The upper two feet was completely bare of anything but the lights they strung last night.

"Need a hand?"

"Well, yes, since I haven't managed to grow another foot since dinner."

Dangerous. Holly Maxwell was a threat, disrupting everything he thought he knew. Mason obliged with the ornaments she'd already picked out, hanging what he could without a stepladder. The angel topper was too risky to try without something to stand on. The last thing they needed was to knock over the tree and have to start over again.

"I guess this is good practice for the trees we have to put up in the barn," Mason said. "Except those all have to have themes."

"Themes?"

He pushed the stepladder toward the tree and stepped up. "Didn't you read my list?"

"I thought I did. Guess I missed the note about that."

"One snowflake tree, one Santa tree, one angel tree. There's a bunch of others, obviously. Maybe I didn't write that all out."

Holly had beaten him to the punch, scribbling away as he propped the angel on the crown of the tree. "Do you remember the chapter it was in?" He shot her a look across the room that implied he in fact did not. "I know, I know. I should just make time and read the book. But every time I sit down to read, at least ten things pop into my head that need attention. And now with people out for the holidays—"

"*This* needs attention." He pointed to her pad of paper. "You're now a hired professional, and you want a happy client to hopefully lock in future business, right?"

"Right." In that adorable, slightly shamed expression and dipped head, Mason recognized a glimpse of the girl she used to be. He'd never thought of her as more than a kid back then. Of course, her grandpa didn't allow any of the hands to think about more with his granddaughters, but now he wondered how many great things he'd missed about Holly by not getting to know her. Befriending her.

"Tell you what. I'll clean up the boxes and totes. You park yourself on that couch and read."

"But—"

"No buts, just read."

"I have to pick up a nutcracker from Jillian tonight."

"Holly," he said, warning in his tone.

"And I need to check the heated water tanks—"

"Bobby already did. Read."

She had to be out of objections she thought he might accept, because she lifted both hands in surrender and dropped onto the couch. She scooped up the novel from the end table and flipped to her spot.

"Good. Stay here. Read."

"Where are you going?"

"To put the empty boxes back upstairs."

"Oh." That cute little blush would be the end of him if he wasn't careful.

Mason grabbed several boxes, enough to risk them toppling and scattering on his trek to the second floor. But the fewer trips he could make up those stairs the better. His leg hurt more than usual, and he didn't like it. The pain was what started the insomnia to begin with.

He fought the limp until he was out of Holly's sightline. But after his third trip, he couldn't take it anymore. Once upstairs, he dropped the pile of empty boxes on the floor in the small hallway and limped to his bed to sit a minute. Blitzen followed him in, hopping up on the bed beside him.

"Hey there, bud." Mason gave him a good rub before he massaged his own leg, hoping to work out the pain. Sometimes it helped; sometimes it made things worse. Tonight, he feared he was making it worse.

"Are you okay?"

Slowly, Mason opened his eyes that had been winced shut in pain. "You can't tell me you finished that book already."

"Finished another chapter." Such innocence in that expression. It softened his annoyance that she followed him. That she caught him in a moment of weakness. "Thought I'd see if you wanted help. Is your leg okay?"

"Yeah." But the fib was sent through gritted teeth. "Just a cramp. It'll pass."

Holly folded her arms across her chest, obviously unconvinced at his poor untruth. "A *cramp*, huh? You never were that great at lying, Mason." She took a few steps into the room, Blitzen's tail wagging at her approach and hitting him in the back. She pointed at the dog. "So *you're* the sock thief."

"Sock thief?"

Holly crouched down and stretched a hand out beneath the bed, coming back with a reindeer sock. "Blitzen. I should've known."

Mason hugged the dog with one arm, winning more tail wags.

"Can I get you anything?" Holly asked.

"I'm okay."

Taking a seat beside him on the bed, opposite Blitzen, Holly said, "Tell me."

"What?"

"Tell me what happened with your leg."

His first instinct was to brush off her request. Find some way to change the subject, or insist she go back to reading that book. But Holly deserved better than any of those things. It might do him good to share his secret with someone. Or it might blow up in his face. He braved on.

"I was on a mission in Afghanistan. Spotted the IED when we were already on foot. Buddy of mine nearly walked right into it, but I pulled him away in time."

"Wow."

"The luckiest detail in all this is that it was poorly constructed. Homemade. It went off, but the shrapnel didn't reach very far." Despite his better judgment, he slowly rolled up his pant leg to reveal the scars he kept hidden from everyone. "Just far enough to get my leg pretty good."

He waited for the gasp, the pity, the *You're so brave*. But Holly Maxwell didn't give him any of those things. Instead, she lifted off from the bed, threw her arms around his neck, and gave him a kiss that made his head spin.

CHAPTER 15

Holly

Holly had only dreamed what it'd be like to kiss Mason. She'd fantasized about such a first kiss nonstop when she was fourteen and completely infatuated. But in all those fantasies, not once did she imagine pouncing and stealing her kiss.

But dang it, when he told her the story of how he was hurt . . . it unraveled something inside her. She wished she could heal his leg, take away his pain. But Mason Montgomery wasn't a man who appreciated pity. No. Holly felt something else entirely. Pride. Proud that she knew such a brave man who acted on instinct and saved both another soldier and himself.

Mason had been willing to sacrifice his life to save another.

At first, her lips met stiff ones. She'd leapt without forethought, without thinking it through at all, much less considering the consequences. When Mason didn't react, she pulled back, ready to flee the room.

But he cupped her cheek and pulled her in closer. Her hand went to his shoulder. The kiss deepened. Until a door closed downstairs, alerting Blitzen, and causing both Holly and Mason to jump apart.

What just happened? She was too chicken to look at Mason. See if he was smiling or wearing that disapproving frown of his.

"Holly, I—"

"I'm sorry," she interrupted. Her gaze locked on the floor. *Is that my missing Christmas-tree sock, too?* It'd have to wait. She needed to bolt. Now. "I shouldn't have done that. It was a mistake."

"It can't happen again. We can't—"

Any hope of him refuting her claim that the kiss was a mistake was gone. She let out a tiny hidden sigh. "I know."

She scuttled down the stairs, almost out of breath by the time she made it back to the living room where a mess of boxes and explosion of decorations still waited. So much to do. Lists coming out of her ears. But she couldn't stay in the house now. She'd go check the horses, or the water tanks, or Norbert. Anything to get away from what just transpired.

"Holly," Amelia nearly scolded. "I've been looking everywhere for you!"

"Just putting away boxes," she said to her aunt.

"Is everything okay?"

"Yep, fine." No way her cheeks weren't as red as those ball ornaments on the tree, giving away everything. Escape was her only viable plan.

"I just got off the phone with—"

"I need to run out to the stables. I'll be back." Holly hurried for the front door, her scarf trailing after her in the commotion. It landed on the front porch, where she left it behind.

The next morning, Holly skipped Mason's home-cooked breakfast so she could sneak away early to the barn. Cowardly, she knew. Her PB and J was not nearly as tasty as that breakfast sausage smelled. The aroma had followed her all the way out the front door and halfway down the steps of the front porch. But she had to get a head start. One that didn't include the man causing her all sorts of confusion.

She *kissed* him. What had she been thinking?

And when she called it a mistake, Mason was quick to agree that it couldn't happen again.

What a mess.

Out at the barn, she hardly had her coat off before she set to work. "Seven trees." She jotted down on her list, *Find the other five.*

Holly worked at setting up the ones she had waiting along the walls of the barn. Admittedly, Mason's list wasn't good at including details like themes, but it had been helpful enough to direct their placement—four on each long wall, two in the front, two in the back.

Other than what she'd written down last night, Holly still had no clue what the other themes were or how they were acquiring the decorations to finish them. It would likely mean a trip to Gillette, but she couldn't fathom where she'd find the time.

Extracting the paperback from her oversized coat pocket, she flipped through pages, hopeful to locate the chapter that described the trees. She'd only managed to finish through chapter five—of twenty-seven—before last night's unexpected, completely unplanned kiss. After that, there was absolutely no possibility of reading. Or sleeping, for that matter.

She located a scene that mentioned the snowman tree, complete with a background of its importance. Holly found herself engrossed in the story, completely invested in Pete's childhood memory of his grandmother only allowing snowmen on her tree, when she heard the barn door slam.

She jumped, a little squeak escaping. The book

dropped to the floor. Blitzen rushed to her side, tail wagging on overdrive.

"You can't cheat and read ahead, you know." Mason wore that smirk that made her heart pitter-patter in drunken patterns. "I know you weren't that far along last night."

Was he completely unaffected by that kiss? *Of course he is.* Holly had always pined after *him.* "You don't read the ending first?" But her teasing came out weak, in a mousey voice. She cleared her throat and crouched down to pick up the book, knocking over an artificial tree she'd just assembled. Could she be any clumsier?

Mason, ever the gentleman, reached out a hand to help her up, then righted the tree. "Missed you at breakfast this morning. Didn't expect you to start without me."

"Just a lot to do. Running out of time, and we don't even have anything for the red and silver tree." An hour drive to Gillette to pick up decorations suddenly sounded like a wonderful idea. It would give them some space. "Think you can get lights hung today? The ones that need to go up in the rafters?"

"You going somewhere?"

Holly swallowed as he took a couple of steps closer. Her traitorous eyes kept landing on those lips. All night long, she fell in and out of sleep, dreaming how it'd feel to be wrapped in his arms. Maybe around a cozy fire. The warmth, security.

She definitely wondered what it would be like if they kissed again. "I have a shopping list."

Mason raised an eyebrow. "Without having finished the book?"

Good point. What amount of bribery would it take for Jillian to help her finish it? She reached for her phone, about to text her friend. "I can always make another trip to Gillette."

"There's time for that?"

Of course there wasn't. There wasn't time for the first. But she needed to get away, even for a few hours. She needed space between them, because her imagination would do nothing but taunt her if he was in close proximity all day.

Mason would never see her as she wanted him to, and even if he did, what would it matter? He wasn't staying. This time next week, he'd be on a plane back to North Carolina. She might never see him again. "There's not time for anything, but that doesn't mean it doesn't get done."

"True enough." He reached out and for a brief moment, Holly thought he meant to take her hand. "Can I see your shopping list?"

"Um, yeah." She handed it over, despite its vastly unfinished nature.

"You willing to let a soldier take a stab at a mission plan?"

Too curious to pretend she wasn't intrigued, Holly said, "That depends."

"On?"

How much time we have to spend together. But she'd never admit that out loud. She'd embarrassed herself enough with that unsolicited kiss. "What your plan is."

He let out a light chuckle. "I bet you can't even go one day without being in total control, can you?" A sparkle danced in his eyes, daring her to argue his too-true point.

"I can, too."

Mason extended his hand, and this time, it very much looked as if he wanted hers. "Prove it."

"How?"

"I bet you a home-cooked meal you can't relinquish control for one day."

Holly stared at his hand, debate skittering through her mind. She didn't want to turn down a challenge. But with so much left to do in so few days, how could she possibly last the day? She *hated* cooking. "This seems rigged."

"Remember who read the book."

She hated to admit he had a point. Knowing full well she might regret it, she said, "Fine."

"Shake on it."

Cooking seemed less daunting than touching Mason. What if she lost control again and threw herself at him? He made it perfectly clear that what happened last night could not happen again. "What are the terms?"

Mason let out a light but deep rumble of a laugh. "I make the plan for what we do about the barn today. The shopping list. Where we go to get everything. All you have to do is go with the flow."

"Until when?"

"Until we get home from Gillette."

Holly fiddled with a tree branch, unable to look him in the eye. *We. Home.* What if he could stay?

"That's not so bad, right?" Mason teased. "If you make it until then, I'll cook you whatever you want for dinner. If you don't, you owe me a home-cooked meal. I'll even let you pick your poison, but it can't be some frozen meal baked in the oven."

Holly stared again at his outstretched hand. Before she could talk herself out of it, she shook. The sensation of his hand made her a touch dizzy, as though she'd been spinning in circles and just now tried to stop. "I might surprise you, you know."

He gave her a wink. "We'll see."

Mason's plan first involved an inventory of everything the Starlight Book Club ladies had gathered in donations. Holly wasn't thrilled to spend her morning laying out Christmas decorations, doing their best to label what belonged to whom. But she could appreciate the organization that Mason put into his strategy.

He studied the clipboard, saying, "Looks like we still need five trees, seven nutcrackers, the mistletoe —which we can't pick up for a couple of days yet— and a mass of tree decorations."

"Is that all?" Inside, she cringed. The money Trish paid for the deposit was used up, thanks to the unreliable heater in cabin number four. She'd have to dig into her own reserve to pay for the remaining decorations until she received the bonus check to reimburse her. Hopefully they found clearance sales this close to Christmas.

"Suppose we should get on the road," Mason added.

Holly busied herself with her phone, checking the weather. Though really, she had been doing her best all morning to keep her eyes—and hands—off Mason, lest she cause a super embarrassing scene. It didn't help that he teased her the same as he had before the kiss ever happened, leaving her to wonder all over again if there was something between them other than her silly teenage crush.

"Maybe we shouldn't go today. Snow's coming."

"Not until this evening. We'll be back before that hits," he said. "Unless you're forfeiting the bet and cooking me dinner?"

Holly felt a twinge of guilt at the ranch chores she wasn't helping with today. Leaving town also meant she'd be late getting back to check on things before the snow hit. "Looks like three or more inches."

"You can't trust those weather apps."

"But—"

"You have a four-wheel-drive truck, Holl."

Dang it, he called her Holl again. She was such a sucker when he did that.

"I'm craving lasagna, in case you need ideas."

She shot him a look that warned him she wouldn't back down easily. Nor was she about to whip up something as crazy as non-boxed pasta noodles. "Let's get on the road." She hurried to the door before she talked herself out of the trip she most definitely didn't have time to make. Even worse, her few hours of peace and quiet now included company.

Norbert greeted them outside the barn door, no doubt unhappy about being excluded. But Holly wasn't willing to risk cleaning up an unnecessary mess in a barn that had taken so well to a new facelift. "We better let them have a few minutes together." She nodded toward the pair that frolicked through the powdery snow as if they'd been separated for weeks instead of a couple of hours.

Holly slipped off her gloves to text Brantley about her trip to Gillette, to ensure there wasn't anything they needed from her before she left.

"I know you like to control everything," Mason

said, pulling her phone away as she waited on a response. "But sometimes you've got to trust that things will get done without you."

Holly'd be lying if she said the words didn't come with a sting, but the fact they were true couldn't be argued. "You mind letting Amelia know we're going?" She wasn't sure she could face her aunt yet without her cheeks turning the shade of the barn.

Stuffing her phone into his coat pocket, he said, "I'll meet you at the truck. Bring that book."

CHAPTER 16

Mason

As Holly scoured store shelves for red ornaments, Mason searched for something silly. Anything that might elicit a laugh, and that smile he enjoyed so much.

He insisted she read during their hour-long drive, and though she obeyed per their bet, he could tell she was wound up tight. She sat too stiffly and kept stealing glances out the window that turned into short trances in which smiles couldn't be found.

"This can't be all their red ornaments." Holly exhaled a long, huffy breath. Light bags hung beneath her tired eyes. "I don't even know what some of these things are." She held up an oddly shaped ornament that slightly resembled what might be either a high-heeled boot or a lamp. She hung it back on its hook.

While her back was turned, Mason reached for a lime green Santa hat with neon orange lining and matching beard. The most hideous thing he'd seen in a while—worse than the misshapen ornament—but he put it on before he spun around toward Holly.

"Did you see any other—" Her mouth hung agape as she registered the sight before her. He wriggled his eyebrows until she burst out in laughter. The sound was music to his ears.

They laughed together until they buckled over, holding sore abdomens. Holly wiped away a tear. "And I thought the remaining ornament selection was bad!"

"Christmas comes in many colors." It'd been so long since he let his goofier side out. It felt good. Refreshing. He'd spent so many years in the army being somber about everything. Despite his comrades telling him he was too serious about everything, he found it hard to relax. Always so much to do, so much to pay attention to. Letting his guard down could get people killed. But here in Wyoming, he could breathe easy.

"It's been a long time, Mason."

He tossed the neon hat and beard back on the shelf. "For what?"

"A long time since I've seen this side of you."

That sideways glance as she walked by him, brushing his shoulder, had a flirty flare to it. He should take a step back, keep his distance. Instead, he reached for the silver garland with Christmas trees from the shelf and snaked it around her shoulders, pulling her closer.

"It's been a long time since the holidays have been enjoyable." It was true. Last Christmas, he'd been in Afghanistan on an air assault mission. The holidays he spent stateside, he burrowed himself at home, tinkering with some old truck in his garage until they were over.

"I'm glad you came home."

When those soft eyes met his own, he swallowed. He meant what he said about their kiss being a mistake. Lawrence would have a field day if he ever found out about it. Besides, Mason was leaving in a few days. It wouldn't be fair to keep kissing Holly under those circumstances, though he wanted to very much.

"I guess Christmas in the desert probably isn't the same, is it?" He watched her eyes fall to the garland that held her captive, only inches away. But she didn't make any move to escape capture.

"The trees are different, that's for sure." He smiled at a fond memory of his unit procuring a palm tree a few Christmases ago and decking it out in lights and ornaments sent from back home. He almost told Holly about it but something held him back. *The need to protect us both from getting too close.*

"Do you miss it?"

The poignant question caught him off guard. "I haven't exactly given it up." It was just a way to dance around the real question, because he wasn't ready to confront that answer. He freed her from her garland trap and tossed it into the cart.

"That'll be perfect for the tree-themed tree." She stepped back so quickly she nearly collided with a display of greeting cards. "I wish I had a creative mind like Trish Meadows. I couldn't write a poem, let alone a book. Then to come up with a dozen different themes for Christmas trees . . ."

Her rambling, though cute, left him feeling a little guilty. A little empty for not having her so close. But it was for the best, he reminded himself. Friends. They could be friends. But nothing more. "I think you have enough red ornaments to cover two trees." Mason consulted the list. "Let's move on to the next thing."

They traveled the Christmas aisles at least three times, careful to keep a physical distance between them as they filled the cart, checking off items on Holly's very detailed list. Yet they still came up short on the last two nutcrackers.

Holly pulled out her phone. "I wonder if there's anywhere in town we haven't tried."

"I'll go ask." While she searched out an answer

on her phone, he made his way to the checkout counter.

"There's a small shop, edge of town. Doubles as a little B and B. Guy there makes custom nutcrackers. He might have a couple left. They sell out every year," an elderly woman wearing a red store vest told him. "Better hurry, though. Clyde closes in less than hour. Might even be gone already with the snow."

"Snow?" Mason searched for a window, but he couldn't see outside from where he stood. How long had they been in the store?

"Already got a couple inches, I suspect, since you've been inside. Roads are slick. It's coming down pretty good."

Holly turned a corner with a full cart and a defeated expression. They should head back, before the weather turned any worse. A truck—four-wheel drive or not—didn't promise the roads wouldn't be dangerous. But he couldn't stand the thought of leaving without their mission completed. They were only two nutcrackers away from having everything they'd jotted on their list.

"There's one more place we can go," he said to Holly, pulling items from the cart and placing them on the counter to check out. "Guy makes custom nutcrackers."

Anyone else might've missed the slightly pale color that washed over Holly's face. Custom meant more expensive. Maybe on the drive home, she'd finally tell him what was really going on with the late nights, wadded papers, and penny-pinching.

As Holly paid for the decorations, the woman behind the register handed them directions she'd scribbled on the back of a receipt. "You two better hurry."

Snow fell in thick, heavy flakes, wetter than the typical snowfall he remembered from his winters in Wyoming. They rushed to empty the cart onto the back seat, and Mason ran the cart back inside the store.

In the truck, Holly plugged the address into her phone. "Weak signal, go figure."

"We'll just have to get there the old-fashioned way." He handed her the receipt slip. "Sounds like it might be a little tricky to find. Think you can navigate?" He'd be plenty busy carving a path through the fresh snowfall the plows had yet to get to.

They worked together, weaving their way to the opposite side of town, through more backroads than Mason would have suspected. The snowflakes fell in puffy cotton balls, but they no longer melted when they hit the windshield. The tracks made by the few remaining vehicles quickly vanished beneath the new layer.

"There, up to the right." Holly pointed at a log sign that read *Clyde and Marcelle's B&B*. "You sure this is the right place?"

"Yeah." Turning into the parking lot, he spotted a

carved and painted nutcracker in the window. It had to be at least three feet tall. "Good, they're still open."

"We better make this quick. I don't like the look of this weather."

Mason left the truck running as they dashed inside, out of the snowy cold and into the cozy warmth of a log structure. A fire crackled opposite the front door, and the aroma of cinnamon wafted through the air. It reminded him they hadn't stopped for anything to eat, and he hadn't allowed Holly to pack a single peanut butter and jelly.

"Come in out of that snow." A woman ushered them toward the counter in the center of the store. "Have a cup of hot apple cider, warm ya up. Grab a snickerdoodle too."

They eagerly obliged, both halfway through their cookies before the woman—Marcelle—asked, "What is it you're needing?"

"Two nutcrackers," Holly answered, wiping a crumb from the corner of her lip. And just like that, Mason wanted to kiss her again. Right there in front of the store owner. But he refrained himself and instead stuck his now-empty hands in his pockets. The sooner they got back to the ranch, the better.

"We have just two left. Right over here." Marcelle led them to the window display. "Christmas is so close, you know. Clyde can hardly make enough to keep in stock through then."

Marcelle stretched her neck out to peer around Mason's arm. "Not sure where he's gone off to."

Holly took the opportunity to reach for the white price tag tied on with a string. Her widened eyes said all he needed to know. Handmade nutcrackers, especially ones this large, wouldn't be cheap.

"Let me go grab him." Marcelle hurried toward the back, leaving them alone for a moment.

"These *are* beautiful," Holly said to him, her voice quiet though there was no way Marcelle could hear them from this distance. "But they're definitely not in the budget."

They'd been to three different stores and cleaned out the nutcracker selection in each. The weather wouldn't allow them to look anywhere else today, and Mason wasn't sure there was anywhere left to try. He didn't think they'd find them unless someone in Starlight was hoarding nutcrackers and had yet to offer them up. "Suppose your book club ladies have interrogated everyone in town?"

"Yeah."

"Clyde, come meet this adorable couple!"

Before Mason could correct him—both he and Holly immediately tried—an older man as thin as a pencil met them at the window display. "Hear ya folks need a couple of nutcrackers. Yer in luck. These are my last ones. Won't make any more until next year."

Mason saw the deep breath from Holly, her way

of preparing herself to deliver bad news, but he didn't give her a chance. "Yes, we need these two." He felt her stare but ignored it. "Last ones in the state, I suspect. We couldn't find any in Starlight either."

"Starlight?" Marcelle repeated.

Holly tugged on Mason's arm, still trying to get his attention. He ignored her, because she wouldn't pay for these. He had more money saved up than he knew what to do with. Easy problem to have when you never went anywhere. "Yes, that's where we're headed as soon as we get these packaged up."

"You're not going back tonight," Clyde said, matter-of-factly. As if he'd already made the decision for them. "Road's closed, didn't ya hear?"

"What?" Holly's fingers dug into Mason's arm. Quite the grip she had there, through his coat even. "When?"

"About thirty minutes ago. Bad accident. Plus the snow now. Semi blocking the whole road. They don't think they'll get it reopened until morning." One at a time, Clyde carried his last two nutcrackers toward the counter, where Marcelle busied herself with wrapping them in several layers of tissue paper.

"Is there another way?" Mason asked Holly.

"Not a reliable one."

"We have a room left," Marcelle offered. "Honeymoon suite, actually. Perfect for a young married couple such as yourself."

Holly almost beat him on that one, but he grabbed her arm. "Just the one?"

"We'll discount it, same price as a regular room. We're full up otherwise," Clyde said. "Weather has everyone extra cautious today and extending their stay."

Mason handed over his card to pay for the nutcrackers. "Add the room on, too."

"Mason," Holly whisper-shouted. "We can't—" Both Clyde and Marcelle ignored the rise in her voice.

"You two just missed dinner, but I'll see about some leftovers," Marcelle assured Mason.

"Thanks, that would be great. We better go shut off the truck," he said, pulling Holly with him. "We'll be right back."

Outside, Holly asked, "What are we doing? We're not *married*!"

He studied her for a beat, those chocolate eyes wide with disbelief, her dark curls fluttering freely below a teal stocking cap. What would it be like to be married to her? The thought struck such a punch he sharply turned away. He never thought he'd be married to anyone. Settling into a normal life . . . it just wasn't his thing.

He set the nutcrackers in the back seat, taking a moment to catch his breath.

"Mason!"

"We need somewhere to stay." *It's a terrible idea.*

If Amelia or Lawrence ever caught wind of this sleeping arrangement, they'd have a hay day. But the alternative was to sleep in the truck or chance even worse backroads. "We can't risk getting stranded on some drifted-over backroad." Four-wheel-drive truck or not, it wasn't a guarantee they'd get far.

"This isn't right, lying to them." Holly nodded toward the store.

"If you want to tell them the truth, I'll sleep in the truck tonight. You can have the room." He wasn't crazy about that arrangement, but he'd do it if he had to. Maybe they'd let him sleep inside the store, on the floor. He'd slept on plenty of hard surfaces in his day.

"No, I'm not letting you do that."

He'd sleep on the floor, let Holly have the bed. His throat grew a little tight at the thought of his privacy invaded. If she didn't know about his insomnia before, she'd likely pick up on it tonight.

"I need to call Brantley."

Mason nodded, hiding his sweaty palms by wiping them on his jeans. "I'll get the room key."

What a right mess. If he hadn't insisted on them going today . . . Mason shook his head. No, Holly would've gone alone. Might've tried to drive home in the snowstorm. This was better than the alternative. They'd head back first thing in the morning, as soon as the road reopened.

He only hoped the Maxwell family forgave the

inappropriate sleeping arrangement forced on them by the inclement weather. But he wasn't too confident everyone would understand.

CHAPTER 17

Holly kicked off her boots by the door to the honeymoon suite, completely stunned at their bad luck. Three inches of snow had turned into quite the blizzard. "You're sure everything is fine?" Holly asked Brantley once more on the phone. "We can try to take a different road—"

"We've got it covered. We've checked on the herds, the horses, the water tanks, the fences. They caught the wolf over at the Livingston Ranch, so that's no longer a threat. My mom has Blitzen, and Jillian stopped by the house and tucked Norbert in. When did you teach that cow to use a doggie door?"

"All the credit goes to Blitzen. Are you sure you'll be good without me th—"

"I'll call you if anything comes up. See you in the morning."

So Holly plopped onto the enormous bed, staring at the lace pattern of the canopy above her head. Mason had gone to wrangle up the promised leftovers, as they'd missed dinner in the commotion. The roads in town were inadvisable for travel, and most restaurants had closed up early as a result.

We don't have time for this. The gala was only days away, the decorations hardly started. If Trish or Lina stopped by, they'd find a barn that looked as though Christmas exploded in it. Through that chaos, they wouldn't be able to see the end result.

"We don't even have the lights up," she muttered to herself. How much sleep would be lost trying to pull this off? If only she'd turned down Mason's control challenge. She let out an ugly sigh at that. She'd have been stranded by herself, probably on the highway. Coming to Gillette was *her* idea, not his.

No matter how much she denied it, it was better that he came along.

She just had to figure out how to survive an entire night with Mason sleeping so close by. Though the room had a few extra features like a small dining table, a stiff reading chair, and a fire-place, it didn't have much floor space or anything as convenient as a couch. There'd be no escaping him until dawn. And even then, they still had to make it back to the ranch.

"Dinner is served." Mason closed the door behind him. He balanced a couple of covered plates in one hand and a paper sack dangled from the fingers of the opposite one. "And dessert."

Holly sat up, raising a suspicious eyebrow. "Leftovers." The alluring aroma, however, did hold promise.

"Pot roast, potatoes, carrots."

Her stomach rumbled. "It does smell awfully good."

Mason set the food on the round table by the window. "She even packed us some snickerdoodles."

"Okay, I'm up." Holly approached the table for two, ready to devour every bit of the haul Mason had been lucky enough to hunt down. When the fog of her hunger delirium cleared briefly enough for her to remember her manners she added, "Thank you."

"Couldn't let us starve, now, could I?" Mason gave her a wink that made her stomach do entirely different things than it had a moment ago.

"Do you think that storm will really clear by morning?"

"Sooner."

Holly slipped into a chair, holding her fork at the ready. If Mason didn't hurry and sit down too, she'd lose any ability to be polite and wait. "Sooner? That sounds promising." Only hunger kept her from reaching for a notepad to make a list for tomorrow.

"Rumor is, the road will be open by eight."

"Eight?" That would never do. It would be well after nine before they got back to the ranch. So many things happened before nine a.m. She might as well call in sick, and Holly Maxwell *never* called in sick.

"Better than being delayed another day, right?" Finally, he sat down, and Holly dove in to her pot roast, savoring the tender meat and its amazing flavor. Her stomach convinced her she hadn't eaten in a week, and stopping was impossible. "This is so good," she said between bites.

"Last of the leftovers, too. We're lucky to come by it." They shared an innocent smile across the table, one of friendship. But something more lingered in that gaze and forced Holly to drop her eyes back to her nearly empty plate. Nothing could come of this. *He's not staying.*

"How's your leg?"

His easy smile transformed into a straight-lipped frown. "Fine."

Okay, so that topic is off limits. She wanted to ask so many more questions about his time overseas. About his life in the military. About his injury.

"Just spit it out."

"What's it like?" Her plate as clean as she could

get it without licking the rest off, she pushed it to the side and went for the bag of snickerdoodles. "Being in the army?"

Mason shrugged, taking his time finishing his portion. As though he'd rather do anything else than talk about his life. Holly wondered what secrets he might be hiding. Wondered if being stranded in a bed and breakfast, alone in the same room, was suddenly such a brilliant idea. "It's hard to explain."

Holly polished off her first snickerdoodle and went in for a second. Despite her concerns, she wasn't about to let him get away with such a dismissive answer. "Try."

"In some ways, it's like working a ranch. Early hours. Work never stops. Always something that needs to be done." He took his time clearing his plate before he said more, but she waited for him to continue. "Lots of training. Missions." He shrugged. "That's the highlights."

Unsatisfied with the generic, too-broad answers, she stole another cookie and returned to the bed. "TV remote's over there." She pointed to a small end table near the very stiff chair. She still had nearly half the book left to read and since they were stranded, now seemed as good a time as any.

"I'm going to take these plates back." Mason left the room without another word.

Holly let out a frustrated sigh. Mason was impossible. She asked one tiny question, and it shut down all the progress they'd made. The lighter, less serious version of the man was gone again. *What secrets are you keeping, Mason Montgomery?*

Holly found sleep all but impossible. Maybe it was the guilt at leaving the ranch knowing snow was coming, or the guilt for taking on the barn project to begin with. How would her grandpa feel if he knew how much had been neglected in her time spent on a complete gamble? Sure, the extra cash could help get them through part of the winter. Even buy them time if it looked as though it might be necessary to ask the bank for a loan. But it hadn't been part of the original idea.

"You always toss and turn this much?" Mason asked.

Embarrassed that she'd woken him with her restlessness, she said, "Just lately."

"Just lately?" he repeated as though he didn't believe it.

"Since we got the worst price for cattle in a decade, and a storm took out ninety percent of our wheat crop." She hadn't meant to let it slip out like that, but in her sleepy, restless state, she didn't have her guard up as high as she needed it. It did feel good though, admitting things weren't perfect, here in the dimness. A small portion of the weight lifted.

"Sounds like a tough year."

"Something like that." Holly tossed onto her other side and hugged her pillow, wishing the answers to all her problems would magically manifest. Maybe a little Christmas miracle to turn things around. Though a lot was riding on the gala's success, it wasn't enough. "Broken equipment, storm damage that insurance wouldn't cover... You name it, it all happened *this* year."

"Does your grandpa know?"

Holly let out a weak, incredulous laugh at that. "Nope. He'll get his report when they get back. Christmas morning. What a present to deliver, huh?"

"I'm sure he'll understand that you did the best you could."

"You *have* met my grandpa, right?"

"I've found that sometimes when things seem impossible, you just have to trust there's a solution. Believe it."

Holly flipped to her back, searching for the lace-patterned canopy. But in the dark room, she couldn't quite make it out. "I want to."

She heard him shuffling on the floor. In this dark, vulnerable hour, Holly craved the comfort of his arms wrapped around her. As much as she wanted to dismiss it as the pining memories of a teenager, she couldn't. She feared she was developing real feelings for the man Mason had become. What would it be like for them to be married?

The thought dissipated as quickly as it manifested. The idea was too foolish to ever take root. Mason wouldn't give up the army to come work on the ranch with her, and she wouldn't give up the ranch to follow him around the world. Wyoming was her home, and the army was his.

"After that ambush, my squad was trapped." The unexpected sound of his voice left her stunned. She assumed from the silence he'd drifted back to sleep. But Mason sounded quite awake. "I was the only one with an injury. We were fortunate not to have any casualties, but we didn't have a way out. The Blackhawk had taken a direct hit on what was supposed to be allied territory. We were low on ammo. No comms to call for backup. We assumed we were as good as gone."

Holly couldn't breathe. She could hardly imagine what that was like, how terrifying it was to face such fatal danger. And yet, Mason was here with her, sleeping on the floor in one piece. "What did you do?"

"Held our position. Had faith." Mason let out a long, drawn-out yawn.

"Faith?" The answer seemed too simple. Too left-up-to-chance. Something that couldn't be added to a list or made part of a plan.

"When our unit couldn't get hold of us, they sent

backup. We didn't expect it due to the nature of . . . things." Mason cleared his throat, but didn't offer details. Holly wasn't sure she could handle them anyway. "We all got out unscathed. It was nothing short of a miracle when we were up against such grim odds."

Unscathed, expect for his leg. "How long ago?"

"Almost a year."

"Last Christmas?"

"Guess it was."

"I'm glad you're here this Christmas. The thought of you . . ." She couldn't complete that. Yes, she cared about Mason. Cared about him too much. "Why would you think your unit wouldn't send someone to find you?" When he didn't answer right away, she added, "Just wondering what you meant by *the nature of things*."

"I'm in the Special Forces," he finally answered. "Some of our missions are classified. Backup doesn't always exist."

Special Forces? "I don't understand. I thought you were a crew chief."

"I was." He yawned again. "Until Paul died."

She'd forgotten how close he used to be with her cousin. Mason was the reason Paul decided to enlist. They'd gone together, only Paul didn't make it home. "Mason, I—"

Her words were cut short by his snoring. Holly

smirked at that, comforted somehow by the peacefulness of a deep sleep she herself longed for. Tomorrow they'd have to hit the ground running to make up for lost time. But tonight, she tried her best to take Mason's advice. *Have faith.*

CHAPTER 18

Mason

"Mason."

Someone called his name faintly, but he couldn't quite figure out where the gentle voice was coming from. The air around him seemed foggy. Dark.

"Mason, wake up."

Wake up?

Something touched his shoulder. Rocked him. A hand. *Someone.*

"C'mon, we have to get on the road."

He blinked a few times before reality set in. His eyes opened, landing on the soft, gentle face of an angel. "What time is it?" Grogginess tugged at him.

He wanted another hour. Maybe two. The exhaustion that gripped him begged for the whole day.

"Seven-thirty. They're supposed to open the road by eight."

Shocked it was so late, he forced himself to sit up. Holly's hand fell away from his shoulder, leaving him to fight the impulse to pull her into his arms. If she slept beside him, he had no doubt he could sleep the day away effortlessly. "That late?"

"Marcelle knocked a bit ago. She made us breakfast. Omelets and French toast. C'mon. Get up."

He pushed to his feet, still stunned he'd slept so long. His last memory was glancing at the clock when he was telling Holly about his unit being stranded. The glowing red numbers placed the time at just before midnight. "Smells good."

He waited for a sense of relief to wash over him. Some weight to lift. He'd been longing for a full night of sleep for weeks now. The one obstacle in his way had finally cleared. He was tired, too. A good sign that he'd likely sleep again. The doc would clear him for duty within the week, he was certain.

"She brought up a pot of coffee," Holly said, pouring him a cup, "but it's nothing to brag about. I might've put four packets of creamer in mine."

"I've had worse." He happily drank the bitter coffee. Anything to wake up before they got on the road. They were down to three days before the big event. Rounding up the decorations had only been a sliver of the work necessary to pull this off.

He watched Holly pick at her omelet, taking only small bites. She kept glancing at the notepad next to her plate. A couple of crumpled pieces of paper lay just out of reach, otherwise he might've taken a look. He studied her gentle features, searching for signs that she might be weary. But with her dark curls pulled up into a ponytail and eyes bright, she looked refreshed as well. Seemed a night away had done them both a favor in disguise.

"Is the ranch in trouble, Holl?" he asked.

Her gaze didn't leave the list in front of her. She scribbled something off, wrote down something else before answering. "We'll make it through most of the winter."

"That bad?"

"Yeah, that bad." Abandoning the list, she cut her French toast into triangular pieces. They remained uneaten. "Grandpa has a reserve for bad years. One I have been trying not to ask to use. It's their retirement money. If we have to dip into that to make it through . . ." She let out a heavy sigh. "It's not fair. Things were in great shape when they left. It's the only way Grandma Charlotte convinced him to go in the first place."

Covering her hand with his own, he caressed her skin with his thumb. "You have to talk to him. He's a reasonable man."

"I hope you're right." She pulled her hand away and slipped out of her chair. "Marcelle said we could leave the dishes. She'll come up, collect them later." Holly shrugged into her coat, dropped the paperback into her pocket, and slipped on her boots.

"Holly—"

"I'm going to get the truck warmed up. Mind dropping off the key?" She slipped out of the room before he could say otherwise.

He wished he could bring her some reassurance. Lawrence was a reasonable businessman. Surely he'd see that this was just a bad year for a lot of things. Nothing Holly could've done about the storm taking out the wheat crop. Or the heat going out in that rental cabin. That Holly continued to march forward and look for a solution should be something the man could appreciate. Admire. Mason knew *he* did.

He hurried to finish his breakfast, knowing full well Holly was ready to go now. She wanted to be first in line when that road opened, and they couldn't do that if he was still nibbling on his breakfast.

Gathering the blankets from the floor and setting them in a chair, he let out another yawn. He could so easily climb into that bed and sleep a few more hours. He almost did, almost forgot where he was, until his phone buzzed in his pocket.

His commander.

Mason stiffened, not sure he was ready for the conversation. A few days ago, he'd have been over the moon to report his progress. After sleeping more than seven straight hours, he was certain he'd be cleared to return to duty. Allowed to sign those reenlistment papers. Today, however, he felt a slight edge of dread.

"Captain Delowery, how are you, sir?"

"Good, good. Holiday bustle and all, you know." His commander wasn't a man of many words. As few as possible when it came to chit-chatting. "Calling to check in on you. See how you're coming along. Any luck with sleep?"

"Yeah, actually." Mason scrubbed a hand through his hair and over his tired face, searching the room for a mirror. No bags under his eyes. Just a mess of the mop of hair. And his beard was as long as he'd ever let it get before. He'd have to shave that off before he returned. "Got a full night last night."

"Really?"

"Yes, sir."

"Good. That's really good to hear." A mixture of voices and an announcement on an overhead speaker filtered through the phone. One kid screamed.

"You headed somewhere for the holidays?" Mason asked, because he wasn't sure what else to say. A week ago, he would've been chomping at the bit to get that reenlistment paperwork ready for him to sign. His leg hurt a lot less these days, too. Everything he wanted was falling into place. Yet something dampened the excitement he should be feeling.

"Wife's from Nevada so we're headed that way as soon as we get out of this awful store. Christmas shopping is not at the top of my list, you know. Usually leave that up to Yvonne, but we're on a tight schedule this time."

Tight schedule. Mason shoved his feet into his boots, snagged the key from the dresser, and headed downstairs. "I'll be heading back next week, couple days after Christmas, I think." His leave form would keep him through New Year's if he wanted. He had as much saved up as the army would allow, considering he never took a vacation anywhere. But staying away that long had never been his intention. Now, he felt conflicted.

"Call me when you get back. I'll see to it you don't have to wait for an appointment."

"Thanks, sir."

"Whatever you're doing, keep doing it, Montgomery. You sound better. Relaxed. Wasn't sure you even knew what that meant."

Mason gave a light laugh as he flew down the stairs with the keys in hand. "Me, either."

"Take care, Montgomery. We'll see you when you get back."

Before he could tell him to have a merry Christmas, the background chatter went silent. He pulled the phone away to see the call had ended. Whether signal or an impatient man, Mason didn't question things.

"Road just opened up." Marcelle handed him a paper sack, no doubt filled with more snickerdoodle cookies. If he wasn't careful, he might get addicted. The woman had a magic touch when it came to baked goods.

"Thanks for putting us up."

"Of course. It was a pleasure to have you, even briefly. You two drive safe now." He nodded and made it almost to the door. "Mason?"

"Yeah?"

"You two make the most adorable couple." Marcelle glanced over her shoulder, her husband working on something behind her. "I wish you many years of happiness together."

"Thanks." He forced a smile before he dashed out into the cold, but his stomach tied in knots. He'd never met anyone like Holly. No one who made him contemplate years together. In his line of work, he was careful to keep everyone at a distance. But now, he wondered if he'd been missing out the entire time.

He could see his breath the instant he was outside, but at least the snow had stopped. "I had to be out cold last night," he said to Holly as he hopped into the passenger seat. He'd offer to drive, but she seemed set on it. Plus, his eyes were fighting to stay open. "I'm usually a light sleeper." Would she be upset if he napped on their drive back to the ranch?

"You were snoring a little bit like a freight train,"

she teased, a twinkle in her eye, as she backed out of the parking spot and went for the road.

"Snoring?"

"I'm afraid so."

Mason smiled a big, cheesy smile. If he'd been snoring all night, that meant good things. He could only hope his nights of restlessness and fitful bursts of sleep were over. "If I start snoring again, just throw something at me."

"Don't tempt me. It might be a snowball."

They shared a brief look before Holly had to turn her attention back to the road. It left Mason more confused than ever. Sometimes he thought there might be something growing between them. Something more than friendship, no matter how much he fought it. Moments like this when she teased him, that flirty edge in her tone made him replay Marcelle's words. What would life be like if Holly was always a part of it?

He bunched up his jacket to lean his head against the window. None of that changed the fact he'd be packing his bags soon. Leaving. Returning to reality. The army still owned him, cleared for duty or not. The thought left his stomach feeling a little bit like it was filled with lead.

CHAPTER 19

Holly

"This is absolutely amazing!" Trish's eyes sparkled with joy as she spun a full circle in the barn, hand covering her mouth. They'd turned all the Christmas lights on and cut the others. Though daylight filtered in through the windows, the effect was nearly the same at it'd be come evening. "I can't believe it. It's a dream come true."

The Starlight Book Club ladies had already descended on the barn, and they were scattered in various areas ogling the decorations. Their smiles and animated gestures left Holly certain they approved.

"All that's left are tables and the mistletoe,"

Mason assured them. "We'll get all that today." The tables would be delivered before dinner, allowing them to set up the chairs currently stacked in the corner.

"Aside from spreading tablecloths and placing the snowman centerpieces, the caterers should handle the rest of the table arrangements tomorrow," Holly added.

"They even found your nutcrackers." Wade, Trish's fiancé, gave her a side hug. They both smiled wide at something special between them. Holly wondered if that little bit had been added to the story for Wade's sake. She supposed Trish garnered inspiration from the people around her.

"Hope you don't mind that I brought him along?" Trish gave a side nod toward Wade.

"Not at all. Why don't you two take a look around?"

"We'll be here," Mason added when Trish hesitated.

"Let me know if you want anything changed or added. There's still time," Holly said as they wandered away. A happy client was the key to future business, she reminded herself, despite the overwhelming urge to pencil in a nap.

Holly slipped her notepad from her back pocket once they set off, checking the remaining items once more.

Pick up mistletoe from Peggy's Petal Paradise

Set up tables, chairs, and tablecloths

Hang mistletoe (day of)

Check lights one more time (day of)

"We did it." Mason gave her hand a quick squeeze. Her heart fluttered in her chest, but whether it was from their near-impossible accomplishment or from his touch, she couldn't be certain.

"Never could've pulled this off without you." The past three days had been a blur, to say the least. Since the moment they arrived home from Gillette, it'd been chaos. Ranch chores, barn decorating, plowing the snow from the parking area, finishing the decorations in the main house. Luckily, Aunt Amelia had been set to cook the meals and keep them fed. Otherwise, they'd have been forced to survive on peanut butter and jelly. Holly bumped Mason playfully with her shoulder. "You still owe me dinner, you know."

"Do I?"

"Yes, you do." She was ready to give him a spiel about giving up control, but she spotted the curve of his smile. "I'll let you know what I decide. Maybe filet mignon or crab legs."

"I was thinking something along the lines of grilled cheese."

"Grilled cheese?"

"Still a step up from PB and J, right?"

"I don't know about that—"

"This event's going to be the talk of the town,"

Aunt Amelia said, closing the barn door behind her. Holly caught a glimpse of the black cow before the door shut. Both Norbert and Blitzen no doubt wanted to see what had become of the space, too. But Blitzen's overly eager tail would cause a path of destruction if set loose in here. "Already heard a couple of rumors of possible wedding bookings."

"Really?" Holly had hoped all along that converting the barn into a venue would provide a long-term benefit. "That's kind of exciting." But considering where the project started and all that'd been overcome in the process, that wish was a little much to hope for. Even as some Christmas miracle.

Amelia slipped off her gloves and shoved them in her pocket. They'd turned up the heat both to bring the barn up to temperature for tomorrow and to allow Trish and the book club ladies a sense of comfort that her guests wouldn't freeze, despite frigid temperatures and a severe lack of insulation. "Hope your grandparents are okay with this whole thing. You know how Grandpa hates surprises."

Holly's enthusiasm quickly dimmed. If the event were a success, there was no guarantee her grandpa would ever get onboard for future bookings. Holly wasn't an event planner, and they didn't have the budget to hire one.

Guilt tugged at her, but she had to stand by her decision. If she called her grandparents now and broke the news, Grandpa still might be fit to cancel the whole thing. She'd have to clean out her savings to pay Trish back. She wouldn't have a dime left of the getaway money she'd need to hide from her shame. "We have any more company?" she asked, hoping to divert the conversation.

"Couple of your cousins got in. They're staying at the hotel."

Holly frowned. "That wasn't necessary."

"You don't have a swimming pool."

"Ah, guess not."

"I'm going to take a quick look around," Amelia said. "This really did turn out neat! Dinner'll be ready by six."

Holly went back to her list, or tried to anyway. But Mason gave her only a moment until Amelia moved out of earshot. "You never told them, did you?"

She shook her head. No point in lying to Mason anymore about matters of the ranch. He knew about as much as he could regarding the true situation she'd hidden from the rest of them. "One of those, 'better to ask forgiveness' situations." At least, she hoped that gamble would pay off. "They won't be home until it's over anyway. I'm hoping we'll have a couple more bookings before tomorrow night's over."

"I see." That straight-lipped frown was back.

"You don't agree?"

"Not for me to decide."

The consequences wouldn't be his to face

either. Though she appreciated Mason's help—she couldn't have possibly gotten this project accomplished without him—she had that burden to face all on her own. She couldn't imagine a single scenario in which Grandpa commended her on her innovative idea. But she hoped in time he'd come around.

She watched Trish and Wade moving about the barn, holding hands. Sharing excitement. Stealing cute little kisses. Holly felt a pang of sadness. That would never be her and Mason. In a few days, maybe less, he'd leave. "Think you'll ever come back?" She tucked the list back in her pocket. "To Starlight?"

"I hope so."

It wasn't the answer she hoped for, but it was more than she expected. "You're always welcome to stay here."

"Thank you. I appreciate that."

"We could use a mechanic," Holly kept on. Never mind that she couldn't afford to hire their own mechanic, though that had been in the original plan before the hail storm. She should stop talking, but words spewed anyway. "You're really good with fixing things. That tractor hasn't run in I don't know how long, and yet you used it to clear the parking lot."

"I'd get that truck back in shape if I had more time with it."

"That truck has given anyone who's tried a run

for their money. But every time I think about selling it, it seems to come in handy for something."

The book club ladies were scattered about the barn, admiring the improvements. Holly smiled at their lit-up faces as they oohed and ahhed over the decorations.

"I'd buy that old truck."

"I'm *not* letting you drive that back to North Carolina."

Together they laughed at that. Holly would miss these moments most of all. "Still have time to come with me to pick up the mistletoe after dinner?" Though she hoped to have one evening of rest before the gala, at least the last task was an easy one. They'd wait to hang it until tomorrow.

"Can't let you finish this project without me, can I?"

Holly smiled at that, wishing she could reach for his hand. Wishing they were the happy couple strolling around the barn, admiring the decorations, sneaking kisses. "Good." Tonight, she had a small surprise in store for Mason. A special sendoff of sorts.

"I don't know how you two pulled this off," Mitzy Collins, head of the book club, stopped by to say. "But don't change a thing!"

"It's perfect," another lady who's name Holly couldn't recall gushed. "I feel like I'm *in* the story!"

"It's true," Trish added. "You've captured all the

most important elements from my novel." She wiped away a happy tear. "It's better than I could have imagined. Thank you, thank you!"

Mason nudged her discreetly with his elbow, a quick look from him saying *See, pays to read the book, doesn't it?*

"I'm really happy you approve," Holly said. Trish would never understand the full meaning of that statement, and that was okay. Because the impossible was about to manifest itself tomorrow night. "No changes or anything?"

"Not a single thing. Once the mistletoe is hung, leave it just the way it is. It's stunning!" She fished in her purse, handing Holly a check. "Here's the rest of it. I know it'll be a success. We're completely sold out!"

"Wow, sold out?" That had to be almost a hundred people if the number of chairs matched the tickets available.

"We'll be back about four tomorrow? I want to do a live online walkaround for my fans."

"Certainly. I'll be here to let you in."

Wade snaked an arm around Trish to wrangle her out the door. She couldn't seem to peel her eyes from her vision come to life. The book club ladies and Aunt Amelia followed, leaving the barn suddenly quiet.

"No matter what comes of it," Mason said to Holly once the door closed behind them, "you should be proud of this, Holl. When I first heard you wanted to throw a dance in here at Christmas Eve, I thought it was laughable."

"You did?"

"You proved me wrong. Very wrong." He touched her arm briefly, letting his hand slide down. "You'll prove your grandpa wrong, too. I have faith."

CHAPTER 20

Mason

Mason had never seen mistletoe before. Only in cartoonish drawings, but never in person. The author certainly loved her mistletoe. They carried two dozen little green bundles to the truck, each tied with decorative red bows, laid out in flat boxes, stacking them in the back seat.

"You sure we have enough?" he teased Holly. They'd been doing an awful lot of that lately. Teasing. Flirting. Acting as though he wasn't going to leave in a few days. Her question about whether he'd come back was a constant thought whispering in his ear these days.

"You better not get too close," she warned,

waving a bundle of mistletoe at him. Her cheeks flashed a light shade of red, but her blushing wasn't as frequent as it'd been when he first showed up. Seemed she'd begun to grow comfortable around him, just in time for him to leave.

"Or what?" He shouldn't. He really shouldn't play this little game over mistletoe.

"I don't make the rules, you know."

He wanted the excuse to kiss her, right here in front of Peggy's Petal Paradise. He'd wanted an excuse for days now, but that didn't mean he should take it. "No?" He took a couple of steps closer anyway, the warning fading to a mere whisper now that he chose to ignore it.

"It's bad luck."

He reached for the bundle in her hand, lifting it above his head. He stepped closer to her, boxing her in between the open truck door and the deserted street, aside from the store owner's car parked two stalls down. "What's bad luck?"

"Not to . . . to kiss if you pass under the mistletoe." That blush was back in full force, her cheeks as red as the bow.

"I guess that leaves us no choice, does it?"

Holly shook her head. "I don't need any bad luck."

"Me, either." The words came out a little shaky. Had a woman *ever* made Mason nervous before?

One hand held the mistletoe above them as he

took the final step. The other reached for her cheek, tracing his fingers slowly along her jawline to tilt her face toward his. He waited, giving her that moment to break this up. To slip away from him and curse them both to bad luck.

Holly stayed, her gaze meeting his then dropping to his lips.

Had his pulse ever raced this fast on a mission? He didn't think so. "To good luck," he toasted, whispering close to her ear. He let his cheek brush against hers, savoring the closeness in this intimate moment. The scent of cinnamon lingered there on her neck.

"Good luck, yes."

He placed a gentle kiss at the corner of her jaw. "If you don't want me to kiss you, I need to know right now."

"But I do." Her innocent answer came quickly. Without thought.

He kissed her on the cheek, his hand caressing down her neck. "I can't stay."

"I know. I can't go with you."

"I know." His lips brushed one corner of her mouth, then the other. "I don't want to hurt you, Holl." Their lips were only an inch apart, two at most. "I care too much."

She made the move, her lips meeting his. Incapable of resisting the allure of the kiss he'd sought all along, Mason moved his lips with hers. His head spun as tiny snowflakes danced around them. His arm ached, but he held it above them anyway. This kiss, deliberate and expected, left him disoriented. He'd remember it when he was sleeping halfway across the world on a cot in the desert.

"Promise me something," Holly said, her lips close enough they brushed his own with her words.

"Anything."

"Promise you won't forget me."

Mason set the mistletoe inside the truck with the rest and drew her into his embrace, holding her too tightly. Desperate to lock this moment into his memory, this feeling of her in his arms, to carry him through the hardest days to come. "I could never do that, Holly. Never."

In this lifetime, no matter where the army sent him, Mason could never erase a woman as remarkable as Holly Maxwell from his memory.

Bells jingled as another customer entered the floral shop, a warning that they needed to get a move on. Though he would proudly tell the world that he kissed the most beautiful woman he ever met, he didn't think the news that they'd been lip-locking downtown would sit so well with her grandpa.

"I'll drive." Holly fished her keys out of his jacket pocket. "We have one more thing to do before we head back."

Intrigued, Mason hopped into the passenger seat without argument. He longed to reach for her hand across the center console, but he feared it would further muddle an already-complicated situation. A single stolen mistletoe kiss was one thing. But if he wasn't careful, they'd both fall too far. They'd both get hurt. "We on some sort of secret mission?"

"Might be." Holly winked at him before she backed up the truck.

"We're not out to steal any nutcrackers or anything crazy like that, are we?"

"No. I'm not eager to get arrested this close to Christmas." She turned down a residential street, and her speed dropped to less than ten miles per hour. "Though, it might be preferable to be in a jail cell rather than face Grandpa."

"Lawrence is strict. A little stubborn. But I don't remember him being *that* bad to work for."

"You aren't his descendent. Seems the expectations rest a little higher by default of bloodline."

Mason couldn't lift his gaze from the speedometer that now registered single digits. "We looking for something?"

"At." Holly reached her hand across the cab, using her soft fingers to turn his cheek forward. Her touch left tingles in its absence. "We're looking *at* Christmas lights."

It still took him a moment to register what she was getting at. But finally, his eyes fell on the houses lining the street, almost all of them decorated with colorful lights. A few had a single strand along the edge of the roof. Others had displays of reindeer on their roof, inflatable snowmen in the yard.

Mason pointed. "That one has enough lights to keep the entire town lit."

"This is only the first street. Wait until we get to Maple. Everyone there treats this like a contest. Rumor is they hire judges, and winner gets a boat-load of money."

"Only in a small town."

For over an hour, they leisurely drove down any residential streets that held a hint of Christmas lights. The town of Starlight, though small at fewer than twelve thousand people, had quite a few roads to offer for their little tour.

"I haven't done this since I was a kid." They stopped outside one house where the lights danced to the rhythm of "Carol of the Bells." "Of course, they didn't have anything quite this fancy when I was ten."

The squeeze of Holly's hand brought him comfort. He didn't want to let go.

"We've been running nonstop since the day you showed up, and I haven't paid you a dime. Figured the least I could do was get a little Christmas light viewing action fit in to our crazy schedule."

"Thank you, Holl." He hadn't thought of his parents in more than an arms-length way in years. He didn't like the emotions stirred up when he had to face that they weren't here anymore. Their lives had been cut short, and there was nothing he could do about it. "I almost forgot what Christmas could be like."

"Can't have that." She slipped her hand out of his and used it to steer around a sharp corner.

"My family used to make a pretty big deal out of the whole thing. My mom . . ." He laughed. "I swear I'd come home from school one day and it'd look like Christmas exploded in our house."

"Even if you have to go back, I'm glad you're here, Mason. For Christmas."

In another lifetime with fewer obligations, missions and danger, he'd marry that woman sitting in the driver's seat. He'd be crazy not to. "Me, too."

CHAPTER 21

Holly

"Really something, huh?" Mason stepped up beside her, snow crunching beneath his boots as he pulled his coat tighter around him. They both stared straight ahead at the barn, filling with guests.

Whatever fate had in store for them, Holly no longer tried to guess. She hated the thought of him leaving, but asking him to stay . . . it wasn't even a possibility. "I couldn't have done any of it without you."

"It kept me busy."

Holly couldn't believe the number of cars, the crowd. Christmas music from a jazz band drifted outside as the barn door opened and closed. If someone had asked her a month ago whether such a feat was possible, she would've laughed long and hard. The barn had been mostly unused except for storage for the past few years. Holly hardly recognized it.

Norbert trotted up to them and stopped, waiting for Holly to scratch him behind the ears. Something he picked up from his best friend, no doubt. "Sorry, buddy. We both know Blitzen would cause too much commotion tonight."

Unease still prickled at the back of her neck, wondering how her grandpa would react to Norbert. No bright ideas had popped into her head as to how to make that situation work, and she feared nothing would. If she had to put him with the other cows, it'd not only break her heart, but Blitzen's as well.

Satisfied with a few pats, Norbert wandered off toward the house, in search of his dinner, no doubt.

"We should probably go in." Mason reached for her hand, already two steps ahead. "Make an appearance and all that."

Holly took his hand, forcing away whispers from reality. Tomorrow morning, she'd no longer be able to hide from it all. But this Christmas Eve night, she refused to let gloomy thoughts invade their night. About Mason leaving, about Norbert, about the ranch, about any of it.

Inside, the glow of Christmas lights illuminated the barn in a magical, golden way. The contrast of the darkness through the window made it all the more special. Holly felt very underdressed in her dark-washed jeans and soft red sweater. But Jillian had reassured her the black boots and decorative scarf really dressed up her outfit.

"It really is like a dream, isn't it?" she whispered to Mason.

Jillian spotted them from a table in the middle and waved them over to join her and Brantley. Holly shrugged out of her coat and handed it to the coat check at the door.

"I can't believe you guys pulled this off!" Jillian grabbed her wrist with an excited squeeze once she sat down. "Holl, you outdid yourself."

Holly winked. "I even read the book." Her eyes traveled the room, taking in the finished product. The tables outlining the dance floor, the band on stage preparing to play another Christmas carol, the mistletoe, the lights, the crowd.

"Great turnout, don't you think?" Mason asked, leaning closer to Holly to say so.

"Amazing."

"You're pretty incredible, you know that?" Mason gently ran his knuckle along her cheek, leaving his finger lingering at her chin. What Holly wouldn't give to kiss him right there, all these people watching or not, she didn't care. "You had a mission, and you made it happen. Despite everything."

"Ladies and gentlemen!" the lead singer of the

band announced. "Grab your partners and fill up that dance floor. We're about to deck this place out in Christmas spirit."

Brantley pulled Jillian to her feet before the announcer even finished, leaving Holly and Mason to follow suit. "Shall we?" she asked.

They danced to half a dozen upbeat Christmas songs that energized the crowd. Holly wouldn't have pegged Mason for someone who could dance, but she'd come to find the man was full of surprises. When she asked him about his leg, he happily told her the pain was nonexistent. Had been for the past couple of days.

"We need to grab some punch," Jillian said, latching on to Holly's wrist and pulling her away from the dance floor. "We'll meet you guys at the table."

Holly expected a string of questions was coming, and braced herself. Jillian wouldn't pry if she didn't care about her. She managed to down a glass of fruit punch before they came.

"So, you and Mason, huh?"

"No." Holly refused to let any glumness in. Tomorrow, she could face reality. Or maybe the day after. But tonight she could pretend they had forever before them. *Forever*. The word struck a chord. She couldn't possibly be . . .

"You always were a terrible liar, Holly. At least around me."

"He goes back in a couple of days. Hasn't even decided *if* he'll come back, much less when that might be." Holly refilled her glass. "I don't want to think about it tonight. We're friends, having a good time. Nothing more."

"The way that man looks at you, Holl, I promise you are not just *friends*."

Holly needed a minute before she returned to their table, because there was absolutely no way Mason thought of her as *more*. They'd been careful to set that boundary.

Sure, they'd shared a couple of amazing kisses. Especially that last one under the mistletoe. But reality had never been subtracted from the equation. Even if Mason liked her, it wouldn't change anything. The army needed him, and the ranch needed her. "He's leaving, and I can't go with him. That's all there is to it."

"You're just going to let him go?"

"What would you suggest I do? This ranch is my home." She could no more leave it behind than Mason could quit the army with a two-week notice.

Jillian patted her on the shoulder. "You'll figure something out, Holl. You always do."

The pressure to find all these solutions bubbled in her chest. Everyone knew her as the person who could solve any problem. Yet all she'd done this year was dig things deeper and deeper in a hole. Every solution she tried only made things worse.

Except the barn.

With everyone at the table occupied in conversation, Holly slipped out the side door for a breath of crisp air. She closed her eyes, sucked in a deep breath, and exhaled slowly. She *could* figure this out. She had to.

"Holly, what is the meaning of all this?"

Her eyes shot open at the deep, stern voice cutting through the sound of merriment from inside the barn. "Grandpa. Grandma Charlotte." She hadn't expected them until morning.

Grandpa's thick brows furrowed together as he scanned the mass of parked cars. "You're throwing a *party*?"

"Holly, dear, why didn't you mention any of this to us?" Grandma Charlotte's expression, illuminated by the glow of light filtering through the window, gave away her confusion. Her disappointment.

"It's not a party. Exactly." Why did she feel like a teenager again? Caught doing something wrong. "It's a booked event."

That didn't make things better, judging by the hardening expression on his face. "Come inside the house."

Holly looked over her shoulder, wanting to tell Jillian or Mason or someone that she'd be gone for a few minutes so they wouldn't worry. But Grandpa marched off ahead of them, clearly out of patience.

The sooner she faced him, the sooner she could make a plan to move forward.

"An event?" Grandma Charlotte asked, craning her neck toward the window to peek inside.

"A local author rented the barn, to recreate a gala from her latest book." Holly braced herself for the difficult conversation that lay ahead with her grandpa. No reason to ruin Grandma Charlotte's night, too. "Why don't you go check it out? Brantley has a table inside, and I know Mason would love to say hi."

Grandma Charlotte looked back and forth between her marching husband and the barn. The curiosity of a Christmas gala won out. "I'll just be a few minutes." She gave Holly a long, enduring hug. "His bark is always worse than his bite, dear."

With great reluctance, Holly stepped into the office. She hadn't even had time to discard the wadded-up papers. At least most were in the trash can. She waited for a scolding on her messy desk.

"I want a report on the year."

"Now?"

"Yes, now."

Holly wasn't ready. Though it was in her nature to prepare for things, she'd been tied up with the gala and keeping up with ranch chores with them down hands for the holidays. But Grandpa wouldn't want excuses. "I am fully prepared to provide you one. The day after Christmas, as we agreed." Though her voice sounded brave, her palms grew sweaty at her sides.

He stood behind the desk, arms folded. Making her feel small. Tiny. *Should I just submit my resignation now?*

"All right. Fine. I'll give you the highlights." Holly folded her arms, too. "It's been the worst year in over a decade. Maybe two." There, it was out. "Broken equipment no mechanic can seem to fix. Hank broke his arm a month ago and hasn't been cleared to come back since. Less than half the calves we had last year. Worst cattle prices I've seen in my time working the ranch. Hail storm took out most of the wheat crop."

"What's this?" He waved a bill at her, the one for the cabin heater she'd left on top of her ledger book. She'd just written the check and put it in the mail today.

"Cabin heater went out with a paying guest inside. It was fix the heater or refund them."

"*Paying* guest? While I was gone?" He slammed the paper down on the desk, a look of anger and disbelief morphing together. "I don't remember granting you permission to add new business ventures to the ranch."

Inside, Holly was shaking. Barely holding back

tears. Outside, she fought with everything she had to maintain a strong front. Lawrence Maxwell didn't much care for crying. He cared for solutions. "I was trying to find a way to make up our losses. The guests pay twice what a hand does for a month's stay."

Grandpa paced behind the desk, his eyes bouncing across the room until they found the window. "And what in tarnation is going on out at that barn, Holly?"

At least that she could defend. "It's been rented out, as a venue space."

"This isn't some party ranch."

"We brought in six thousand dollars."

That stopped his pacing for a brief moment. "No way that barn magically fixed itself up. How much in expenses? Don't go telling me you found some elves from the North Pole to do it for free, either."

Holly grabbed her notepad off the desk and flipped to her rough draft for the event's profit and loss. One she'd planned to have typed up and perfected the day after tomorrow for her formal presentation. "Once I deposit the last check, we'll have made two thousand and twenty-seven dollars in profit."

"What about the heating bill? The electric?"

"I added in estimates." She dropped the notepad on the desk for him to review, but he hardly glanced at it.

"What about labor?"

"I didn't take anyone from their regular responsibilities. Didn't hire anyone, either. Mason and I did—"

"Mason?"

"Montgomery. He's been staying here."

"I know that. You didn't *pay* him? We don't put our guests to work, Holly."

"He asked to help. Refused to be paid."

"Is everything all right in here?" Grandma Charlotte stepped across the threshold, a sweet smile on her face. Years living in this house taught Holly that the woman was never oblivious to her husband's tempers, nor was she rattled by them. "I made a pot of coffee. Why don't you both come in the kitchen?"

Tension thick in the air, they followed Grandma Charlotte into the kitchen, sitting on opposite sides of the table in the window nook. A table Holly hadn't used the entire time they were gone, aside from the meals Amelia cooked for them.

"The tree looks lovely, dear," Grandma said, pouring fresh coffee into a mug and sliding it to Holly. "You two did a great job."

"Thanks." The three sipped their coffee in strained silence for several minutes. "I didn't tell you about the barn because I wanted to prove myself first. We need the revenue stream, and when the opportunity arose, I didn't want to turn it down."

"Two thousand dollars doesn't do much in the grand scheme of things." The bite was still heavy in his tone, but he'd quieted some since their standoff in the office.

"I've already had someone request to rent it out for a wedding in the spring."

"How lovely," Grandma Charlotte chimed in.

"You resigning your position as ranch manager to become an event planner?" The jab landed its expected sting.

"No."

"Then the answer is no."

"No?"

"I'm not running some party destination here. This is a working ranch." Grandpa pushed back in his chair and stood. "I'll be taking over operations tomorrow morning. If you want to stay on as a hand, you better be in that barn on time."

"But—"

"Is that a *cow* in my window?"

Being demoted no longer felt like the worst thing about tonight. "Yes." No matter how many times she'd practiced explaining Norbert to Grandpa, it never ended with a positive result. "His mother didn't take to him. Almost didn't last the spring."

"I don't care what his story is. Put him in the pasture."

Grandma Charlotte's eyes went from Holly to Blitzen sitting at the window, staring at his friend. Holly wished she knew what to say, what to do. Wished there were some way to protect Norbert and

Blitzen's friendship. She contemplated kidnapping him but had no clue where they'd go.

"It's Christmas Eve," Grandma Charlotte said, her voice gentle. But the moment her husband objected, she steeled her tone. "The calf can go back to the pasture day after Christmas. Not a minute sooner."

Grandpa grabbed his hat from the kitchen counter and stomped all the way to the front door. He was likely headed for that old truck Mason had tinkered with. Last she knew, it wasn't running reliably. But they heard it fire up, and Grandpa drove off.

Holly tried unsuccessfully to hold back tears in front of her grandma. "I bought you some time with Norbert, but not much."

"How do you know his name?"

"Your friend Jillian mentioned something about a video. Does he really play soccer?" She glanced to Blitzen. "With him?"

Wiping away a tear, Holly shrugged. "They're besties."

CHAPTER 22

Mason

When Holly didn't come back to their table, Mason knew something was up. He'd been antsy with concern since he watched her slip out the side door without a coat. Only Charlotte taking a seat at their table kept him from looking for her.

"It's so good to see you, Mason." She wrapped him in one of her legendary hugs. "My, would you look at this old barn. No amount of imagination I possess could ever have dreamed this up!"

"Holly and Mason did all this," Jillian said. "Cleaned it out, fixed it up, decorated. Isn't it wonderful?"

Mason had the nagging feeling that Holly was being told right now how *not* wonderful it all was.

Charlotte's hand covered his shoulder, as if to hold him in his seat. Though he could easily escape, he heeded her warning. Holly was strong. She didn't need anyone to fight her battles for her. "They need some time."

He nodded, forcing himself to sit through another half-dozen songs before attempting to excuse himself to go back to the house. But at Amelia's insistence this time, he stayed until the event concluded. "Someone has to make sure the lights are turned out when it's over," she told him.

Mason had hoped Holly would return to complete that task, if not to talk to the party's hostess. But with the last light unplugged, there was no sign of her. Bringing the coat she'd left behind with him, he trudged through the snow—a shortcut, he assured himself—back to the house.

Searching downstairs turned up no sign of anyone except Grandma Charlotte in the living room, snoozing in a recliner. Had he waited too long? The last place she could be was in her room, and if that was the case, he'd let Holly be tonight.

He passed by the office once more to ensure she hadn't snuck back in there while he was in another room. The light was still on, but the room sat empty. Her notepad lay sideways, on top of her ledger book. It drew him closer. He'd spent too many nights awake wondering about those balled-up pieces of paper to ignore them now.

The numbers scribbled in purple ink showed the Christmas Eve gala netting a profit. So why wasn't there a celebration? At least coffee in the kitchen? A couple of wadded papers teetered at the edge of the desk, as though someone shoved them in the general direction of the trash can but they hadn't quite reached. Unable to contain his curiosity any longer, Mason opened one up.

He discovered a list of ideas to bring in revenue—anything from petting zoos to hayrack rides to car washes—but Holly had crossed through several of the items.

Unfolding another one, he found the same thing. More ideas, much the same. Bake sales, craft fair, horseback trail rides. He flattened it out and placed it on top of the other before bravely diving into the trash can with one hand. Dozens of these balled-up notepad sheets revealed the same secret: Holly had been trying for weeks, maybe months, to think of ways to recover their losses.

Surely Lawrence could appreciate the amount of thought and hours of lost sleep she'd poured into this ranch. Holly loved it here.

His heart ached a little at that revelation. She would never leave Starlight to follow him from duty station to duty station, and he'd never let her. This place meant too much to her. A man gone as much as he would be couldn't let a woman sacrifice everything to wait for him between covert missions. The sooner he left, the easier it would be on them both.

"Mason, you're still up?" Charlotte yawned from the doorway.

"Looking for Holly."

"She went to bed. Rough night." Halfway turned around in the doorway to leave, she added, "Why don't you let me fix you a cup of hot cocoa."

Remembering his manners on the way to the kitchen, he asked, "Have a nice trip?" He hoped he could focus on her answer, because his thoughts were in a whirl about Holly. Mason wanted to fix this. Wanted to tell her grandpa what an amazing person she'd become and how much she loved this ranch. Surely he had to change his mind about things.

"Yes, quite lovely." She handed him a cup, seemingly uninterested in discussing her trip. "You love her, don't you?"

He nearly spit out the cautious sip he'd taken. "What?"

"It's okay, maybe you haven't figured it out yet. But you will." She left him alone then with her odd proclamation and his thoughts. Mason couldn't possibly *love* Holly. He cared about her a great deal, admired so many things about her. But *love?* He had sworn he'd never let himself get that close to anyone.

"I can't possibly . . ."

Holly

Christmas morning, Holly did something she'd never done before. She took a day off. Her grandpa gave all the hands vacation days, Holly included. Until now, though, she'd never used one.

She waited until Grandpa was out at the stable delegating assignments before she slipped out of the safety of her room. Filled paper towel carton in hand, Holly made a beeline for the front door.

"Going somewhere?" Aunt Amelia asked before Holly could get her boots on.

"Moving into one of the cabins." Their first guest had checked out two days ago, and they didn't have it booked again until February. That gave Holly time to figure out what to do about the ranch and her living situation. All she knew now was that staying in this house wasn't an option.

"Need some help?" Mason asked, stretching from the doorway.

"I thought you'd be working."

"A guy needs one day of rest, right? Figured Christmas was as good as any day to choose." He took the box from her and headed toward the door. Together, they loaded the truck with her belongings.

As the last box was settled inside the truck, Mason asked, "Does your grandpa know you're moving out?"

Holly shook her head, refusing to make eye contact as they drove down the winding road to the quiet cabin. The entire thing was hardly bigger than the bedroom she had in the main house, but it would be peaceful here. No one questioning her loyalty or work ethic. "I'll pay him what the writer paid. He can't turn that down."

"Didn't go so well last night, huh?"

Holly put the truck into park and fished a cabin key out of her pocket. It dawned on her that they hadn't talked last night. "Nope."

Inside, she set the first of several boxes on the floor. "I hope Blitzen likes it here. It's quite a bit smaller than he's used to." She'd go back for him once everything was moved in and unpacked. Maybe sneak some dinner leftovers with her on that trip, as this fridge was as empty as the one at the ranch had been. And she'd forgotten to swipe her peanut butter and jelly ingredients for the move.

"Blitzen will be happy just to be with you."

"This cabin has a small enclosed porch in the back. I can leave the door open for Norbert." At that thought, a tear threatened to fall.

"Hey." Mason caught her, despite her best attempts to hide her emotions from him. He pulled her into his arms and held her there for several long minutes, rubbing her back. "It'll all work itself out, Holl. Somehow, I know it will."

"I have to put Norbert out in the pasture tomorrow."

He hugged her tighter. "I wish I could stay longer. Help you figure out a plan."

"Wait, you're leaving?" She wriggled out of his embrace, feeling betrayed. She was certain they had at least a couple more days. "On *Christmas*?"

His usually blank expression turned a shade glum. "I have to get back. Brantley's taking me to the airport this afternoon."

Holly wasn't ready for more bad news. Not this close to the blowout she had with her grandpa last night. That the army needed him back on Christmas Day left her feeling completely defeated. "I could drive you."

"We both know that's not a good idea." He reached for her, pulling her in for what felt like their last embrace. Her arms trembled as she held on tight, soaking up the memory of this moment. As much as she wanted to deny it, delaying his departure any longer would only leave them both hurting more in the end.

He kissed her slowly, tenderly. Warmth filled her clear to her toes. It was quite possible she was in love with this man who might never come back. "I wish you could stay."

"I'll always remember you, Holly Maxwell. For as long as I live."

CHAPTER 23

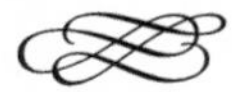

Holly

"You can't hide out here forever." Jillian sat beside Holly on the loveseat that barely fit in the cramped cabin. The loveseat Blitzen claimed for his bed their first night in the new place. "Sooner or later, you and your grandpa will have to sort this out."

Holly stared out the window of the back door at Norbert's blanket. The one Blitzen had chewed up as a puppy. "I have to take him out to the pasture today." Her stomach twisted in painful knots at the thought of breaking up the duo. "I knew someday . . ."

"Don't be so hard on yourself, Holl."

"If I don't do it, someone else will. Grandpa's way of teaching me a lesson."

"Hey, hey. Stop those tears this instant." Jillian was on her feet, waving an envelope at Holly. "I have something that'll dry those puppies right up."

"What's this?'

"Open it."

Holly couldn't fathom what surprise the envelope might hold. All she knew was Mason wasn't inside.

"He hasn't called?" Jillian asked when Holly let the envelope lay limp in her hands.

"No, and I don't think he will." It was better this way. A clean break. It was easier to let him go. Keep the memory of their time together close to her heart, but not hope for a future that could never be.

"I'm sorry, Holl. I wish there was a way it could work out."

She dropped the half-opened envelope in her lap with a sigh. "Me, too."

"If you don't get that open, I'm going to do it for you."

"Okay, okay." Holly tore at the rest. She unfolded the letter inside, printed on thick cream paper and quite official, judging by the letterhead. A slip of paper sailed to the floor. "What is this?"

"Just read." Jillian picked up the paper and dropped it on the armrest.

"We're pleased to inform you that your video *They're Besties* has won first place—" Holly snapped her head up at Jillian. "What video?"

"The one I took and sent in on your behalf."

The pieces were still fuzzy and unassembled in her mind. "I don't understand."

"Of Blitzen and Norbert playing soccer. I shot some video a couple weeks ago because I knew you'd never get around it to. Then I sent it in to a contest, and you won!"

Holly picked up the slip of paper on the armrest, discovering it was in fact a check. "Ten *thousand* dollars?"

"Isn't it great?"

"I can't take this."

"Sure you can. It's made out to you."

"But—"

"No buts. You're the one who saved Norbert and allowed him the chance to befriend your dog. This is all you, Holly."

"Norbert." Holly had tried making a list of all the possible ways she could keep Norbert from being treated like every other cow—because he most certainly was not like any other—but she'd fallen short. All her ideas were terrible, much like the endless lists of ideas to bring money in to the ranch that she'd balled up in the office. *Until now.* "Norbert!"

Holly yanked her keys off the counter and sprinted to the door.

"Where are you going?"

"To see a man about a cow."

Holly hadn't faced her grandpa since Christmas Eve night. She'd used another of those neglected vacation days to get settled in her new place today and figure out what she was going to do. Though she was not above being a ranch hand, it wasn't her dream. If Grandpa wouldn't let her keep her position as manager, she'd have to find another dream to chase.

"Holly, what a pleasant surprise," Grandma Charlotte greeted her in the foyer. "I was just leaving. Heading to the store. Join us for dinner tonight?"

Though her first instinct was to say no, Holly relented almost immediately. Her grandma had done nothing wrong. "Of course."

"Great! See you at five-thirty."

Though confronting Lawrence Maxwell would never be an easy task, no matter the circumstances, Holly wasn't shaking as she had been the other night. She knocked on the open office door before she could allow any emotion like reluctance or fear to hold her back. She waited for him to look up.

"Decide whether you're coming back to work anytime soon?"

"I want to buy Norbert."

That caused Grandpa to set down his pen and close his ledger. "Excuse me?"

"The calf. I want to buy him."

"Don't be ridiculous. He's a *cow*, Holly."

"And I'm willing to pay well above market price for him."

Grandpa sat back in his chair, folding his arms across his chest. "Why?"

"Does it matter?"

"I thought I taught you better than to name our livestock. We can't afford to get attached to the animals that are responsible for our livelihood."

Holly slid the check across the desk. "Then it would be foolish not to accept my offer for Norbert."

Grandpa's eyes widened. "What's this?"

"Norbert's not like any other calf. He's so *unlike* any other cow, actually, that he won a contest. If you watch the video, you'll see." At least Holly was gambling that he would, because in her haste, she'd not had a chance to watch it herself. But anyone witnessing a calf playing soccer with a golden retriever couldn't deny that Norbert was special.

"Take a seat," Grandpa said.

Fighting eagerness to have her offer accepted and guarantee Norbert's protection, Holly reluctantly dropped into the stiff chair facing him. She'd sat in his chair every day for an entire year without fail. Tracked the numbers. Planned the next day.

Searched for answers when things fell short. It felt strange to be back on this side.

The fear that she might never sit in that seat again left her throat a little constricted. She swallowed through it.

"Are these yours?" Grandpa dropped a pile of wrinkled notebook pages in front of her.

"Where did you—" But of course she'd left in such a hurry that she'd not bothered to clean up her mess. "These were for the trash. They're just a bunch of worthless ideas."

Grandpa leaned his elbows on the desk. "It wasn't the best homecoming reception to show up and find a giant party happening on my property, you understand. You didn't tell us—"

"I'm sorry," Holly said. The reasons didn't matter why, not to Grandpa. They were mere excuses. But the apology was necessary if they had any hope of moving forward.

"It gave me the distinct impression"—he swallowed—"that you didn't take your responsibilities seriously the entire time we were gone." He held up his hand when Holly tried defending herself. "Then I found these lists. How many hours have you spent trying to solve this puzzle, Holly?"

"A few."

"I've gone through the ledgers. The numbers are spot on. Reflect an accurate picture."

Yeah, of the disaster of a year we've had. "I care a

great deal about this ranch. It's our legacy, Grandpa. The barn . . . it was a last-minute idea to add revenue to our bottom line. Buy us a little time. A gamble? Sure. But it paid off."

He let out a heavy, grumbly sigh. "I know. I've had three calls just this morning about future rentals."

"Wow."

"Look . . . the other night . . . I acted a little rashly. Your grandma made sure I knew just how much."

It was likely the closest thing to an apology she'd get, but she still didn't know where things stood.

"You've had some good ideas, Holly. Turning empty cabins into long-term rentals was a good one." He fiddled with the stack of papers in front of him. "Some years are worse than others. That's how it goes in this business. But you haven't given up. You didn't call me to ask how to fix things. You did that yourself."

"I tried."

"There're some good ideas in all this, you know." Grandpa riffled though the stack. "We can do hayrack rides in the fall if we plant a pumpkin patch. We have the room."

"Really?"

"Offer sleigh rides in the winter. Sure, there're a couple extra horses we can spare."

Holly was certain she was trapped in a dream,

because the man sitting across the desk couldn't possibly be her old-fashioned grandpa. "I don't know what to say."

"You've remembered the most important thing I taught you. Always be on the lookout for how you can grow and expand your business. A lesson I didn't realize I wasn't following myself lately. You've been thinking outside the box this whole time."

"We can keep the barn as a venue space?" she asked, hopeful.

"If you'll stay on as manager, yes. But you're responsible for all that until we can make room in the budget to hire someone else. You won't get out of any of your other responsibilities, either."

She hopped out of her chair, rushed around the desk, and threw both arms around him before he could object. The man was stingy with his hugs, but Holly was going to get one regardless. "Thank you, Grandpa."

"Consider it my Christmas gift."

The check had fluttered to the floor in her windy dash around the desk. Holly picked it up and handed it to him. "I was serious about Norbert. I want to buy him."

Grandpa stared at the check long and hard before he finally reached out to take it. "Deal. The funds will go into a separate account. One you can use to fund some of these ideas of yours. Does that sound fair?"

"Yes!" She only wished Mason were here to witness this Christmas miracle.

CHAPTER 24

Mason

Cleared for duty.

If Mason hadn't heard it with his own ears, he wouldn't have believed it possible. He waited for the thrill to kick in. Reenlistment paperwork waited for him to sign. He could head overseas for another mission within weeks.

But the only feeling he could identify was confusion.

For the first time in his life, the answers weren't clear. He grew up knowing he'd join the army. It was in his blood. And when being a crew chief and helicopter mechanic wasn't enough for him, he knew he'd advance. Despite the low acceptance and high fail rates, Mason made it into the Green Berets on his first attempt.

Now . . . he wasn't quite sure what he wanted. He *should* want to get back to the action. It was all he ever wanted.

He met his commander in his office, saluted, then handed over the paper proving he got the needed medical clearance.

"Guess that ranch really did the trick, didn't it?" Captain Delowery clapped him on the back. "It's good to have you back, Montgomery."

He'd been sleeping through most nights since he and Holly were stranded in Gillette. At first, he gave the credit to long hours of manual labor. The relaxing atmosphere of a ranch at the edge of a small, isolated town. But days after he left the ranch, he realized it'd been Holly all along.

"You ready to sign away another six years?" Captain Delowery reached for the phone, ready to make the call. They could walk across the street in minutes and Mason could sign on the dotted line. And just like that, he'd be tied up for another six years.

"Let's do it."

This time, Mason didn't tell anyone he was coming.

He hadn't talked to anyone other than Brantley

since he left on Christmas Day, and even that was only to report he'd made it back to base in one piece.

Uncertainty tied his stomach in knots. What if he made the wrong choice?

Parking in front of the main house, he searched the property for Norbert. He didn't see the black calf anywhere, and his heart tightened with fear. He'd tried to keep faith that Holly would find a solution, but Norbert's absence concerned him.

"Mason, what a pleasant surprise." At his knock, Grandma Charlotte ushered him inside before he could say more than hello. She pounced at him with another hug. "I didn't know you were coming back so soon!"

"I didn't, either."

"We're a couple hours out from dinner. Did you want a snack? Coffee?"

"No, thanks. Hey, what happened to your porch ornament?"

"Norbert stays out at the cabin, where Holly moved. She bought him free and clear, so needless to say, he's a pretty happy guy."

Ah, Norbert hadn't been banished to the pasture. Mason felt relieved to hear that. "Is Holly—"

"She's in the office. Go right on in."

He smiled at that news. Whatever had transpired in his absence, Holly and her grandpa obviously worked things out.

Each step down the hallway took him closer yet

left him feeling more nervous, like a teenager with a crush. Only, the emotions he felt for Holly Maxwell were so much more. He'd realized it as the pen hovered above the reenlistment paperwork. Her smile flashed in his mind, that beautiful laugh echoing. He wanted to hear that laugh all the time, not only as some fading memory.

He knocked before he lost his nerve. "I'm here about a job. Heard you might be in need of a mechanic."

"Mason?" Holly stared as though she wasn't quite convinced it was really him. "You're back. I don't understand. The army—"

He stepped into the office, boldly making his way around the desk. "They cleared me for duty."

"That's great news!" Her enthusiasm, though he was certain she wanted to be genuine, didn't reach her eyes. "How soon—"

"I'm not going back."

"I don't understand." She fumbled her way out of her chair, possibly as nervous as he was for this encounter. "I thought I'd never see you again."

He slowly pulled her into his arms, holding her head close to his heart. "I thought I'd never see you again either, and it was the worst thought possible."

"You didn't desert—"

Mason laughed at that. "Of course not." He loosened his embrace so he could tilt her head up toward him. "I have a month left before my enlistment expires. I couldn't sign the extension. The thought of another six years— You could marry the wrong guy, Holly. I couldn't have that."

"But you love the army."

"I do. I did. But I love you more."

Her gasp of surprise was the most adorable thing he'd heard in ages. "You do?"

"I'm serious about that mechanic job. A life on a ranch, tinkering with tractors and trucks . . . it sounds like the change of pace I need. I served ten good years. Gave the army the best of me for a decade. I'm ready for the next adventure. With you."

She kissed him then, her arms wrapping around his neck. "I love you, Mason. I tried not to, but that didn't work out so well."

"I'm kind of an irresistible guy." He went in for another kiss, this one longer.

A little breathless, Holly teased, "You still owe me dinner, you know."

"I'll cook you dinner every day for the rest of your life if it'll save you from your peanut butter and jelly obsession." He kissed her deeper than ever before, sealing the deal.

The Starlight Cowboys series:

Cowboys & Starlight (Book 1)

Cowboys & Firelight (Book 2)

Cowboys & Sunrises (Book 3)

Cowboys & Moonlight (Book 4)

Cowboys & Mistletoe (Book 5)

Sign up for Jacqueline Winter's newsletter to receive alerts about current projects and new releases!

http://eepurl.com/du18iz

ACKNOWLEDGMENTS

To my amazing critiquers, Nikki, Shanon, and Dorie: Thank you so much for your willingness and flexibility to work on such an erratic schedule. Your feedback was invaluable as always!

To the Howells Book Club: Months ago I promised I'd have this book done in time, and on those days I really wanted to throw in the towel, I remembered you. Thank you for the motivation you didn't even know you gave me <3

To my production team, EJ, Brenda L., Michelle, and Brenda W.: My stories always shine because I have such amazing team behind me, helping me each step of the way. I appreciate you all more than you know!

To Husker: As always, thank you for your patience while I poured hours into another book.

You've been a real trooper through this new path, and I promise treats and walks aplenty!

To Andy: Your support means the world to me. Thank you for putting up the Christmas tree and playing Christmas music and movies when I needed a little extra inspiration.

ABOUT THE AUTHOR

Jacqueline Winters has been writing since she was nine when she'd sneak stacks of paper from her grandma's closet and fill them with adventure. She grew up in small-town Nebraska and spent a decade living in beautiful Alaska. She writes sweet contemporary romance and contemporary romantic suspense.

She's a sucker for happily ever after's, has a sweet tooth that can be sated with cupcakes. On a relaxing evening, you can find her at her computer writing her next novel with her faithful dog poking his adorable nose over her keyboard.